This
Strange
and Familiar
Place

17.99

This Strange *and* Familiar Place

a SO CLOSE TO YOU *novel*

RACHEL CARTER

An Imprint of HarperCollinsPublishers

HarperTeen is an imprint of HarperCollins Publishers.

This Strange and Familiar Place
Copyright © 2013 by Full Fathom Five, LLC

Library of Congress Cataloging-in-Publication Data
Carter, Rachel (Rachel Elizabeth), date.
This strange and familiar place : a So close to you novel /
Rachel Carter. — First edition.
    pages   cm
Summary: "Lydia Bentley will do anything to fix the
mistakes she made in the past, like losing her grandfather in
time—and the only way she knows how to begin is by time
traveling to 1980s New York with Wes, posed as a Montauk
Project recruit."— Provided by publisher.
    ISBN 978-0-06-208108-7 (hardcover bdg.)
    [1. Time travel—Fiction. 2. Experiments—Fiction.
3. Grandfathers—Fiction. 4. Missing persons—Fiction.
5. Science fiction. 6. Montauk (N.Y.)—History—20th century—
Fiction. 7. New York (N.Y.)—History—20th century—
Fiction.] I. Title.
    PZ7.C24783Th   2013   2012031814
[Fic]—dc23   CIP
                                              AC

Typography by Alison Klapthor
13 14 15 16 17 LP/RRDH   10 9 8 7 6 5 4 3 2 1
❖
First Edition

To my mother, Terry Gurdak-Carter,
for believing in me even when I don't

CHAPTER 1

My eyes open. The room is dark and filled with shadows. I blink once, twice, and then sit up quickly, my gaze falling on the window near my bed. The early-morning light outside is gray. The tops of the trees sway back and forth in the slight wind. I see a bird fly past, a smudge of color that disappears almost as quickly as it comes. But the windowsill is bare. There's nothing there. Just like yesterday, the day before, and the day before that.

I pull back the sheets that have tangled around my legs and automatically reach for the lamp on my nightstand. My hand falls out into nothing. Right. There's no table there now. I keep forgetting.

I stand up. The floor is cool, and the house is silent, even though it's Saturday morning. I wonder where my parents are, and I picture them standing in the kitchen near the stove, smiling as my father buries his face in my mother's neck. But that's a lost image now, and I push it away as I walk over to my desk. It is covered in papers and books, no longer neat and clean, though I have managed to carve out some space in the corner. The small surface has three items lined up in a row: a shell, a wilted dogwood flower, and a red oak leaf, the kind of color you only find on a tree in autumn.

I reach for the flower but stop before I touch the browning, crumbled petals, afraid it will break apart in my hands. Instead, I pick up the shell. It is pink and curved and hollow. I close my palm around it and feel the sharp edges dig into my skin.

It's from him, I know it is.

Three different items. Three different times I've woken up to find something perched on my windowsill. The first one, the shell, came a few days after I arrived back in 2012. The flower was a week later, almost to the day. The leaf came during week three. By then I was expecting it, and I tried to stay awake all night, every night. But I was so tired and he still didn't come and by Wednesday I couldn't hold out anymore. I fell asleep in the late hours, and when I woke up the next morning it was there, bright and bold against the chipped white paint of the window.

The fourth week, I vowed to wait for him. I slept during the day, barely able to make it through my shifts at my father's hardware store. At night I sat on my bed facing the window, a cup of coffee balanced on the blanket in front of me. If I fell asleep for even a second, I'd jerk awake, my hand pressed to the pocket watch that swung on its chain over my heart. But it was pointless. He never came.

This week, the fifth week, he still hasn't come. And I'm starting to worry and wonder.

When I close my eyes, I see him on the beach leaning over me in the moonlight. I smell him sometimes, pine needles and the earth after it rains.

I have to believe that he's the one leaving these things for me. I have to believe that he still cares. That someone who knows *me*, the real Lydia, still cares.

Here is what I tell myself: he left the shell as a reminder of that night by the ocean. The flower from the tree in my yard, to show he's close. The leaf, to remind me of what he is—someone capable of finding autumn in the height of summer. And maybe that's why there has been nothing since then. Maybe he has delivered his final message—that his life is too different, that we can't ever work—and now he has left me here in this strange but familiar place.

I almost hope this is the reason. Even though it will break my heart, it's better than the alternative. Because the other thoughts are too terrible to face, questions I only ask myself in moments like this, in the small hours of the morning when the world feels quiet and still and empty.

What if he's lost somewhere in time? What if the

Montauk Project has finally used him up and he's gone forever?

Wes.

Where are you?

I have always loved mystery. It was what made me want to become a journalist. It was why I walked into that open bunker at Camp Hero, and why I kept walking through those endless white corridors. I had to find out what was down there, just like I had to solve the mystery of what happened to my great-grandfather, Dean Bentley, in 1944.

And I did solve it. My grandfather was right: There *is* a secret government conspiracy hiding under the ground at Camp Hero, a state park at the far eastern end of Long Island. The Montauk Project is real, they have been experimenting with time travel for years, and they'll do almost anything to keep it a secret.

If the Project ever found out that I traveled back to the World War II era, I would be dead. I'm only alive now because of Wes. But by going back to 1944, I changed something—though I don't know what—in the past, and in this time line my grandfather has been missing for more than twenty years.

Another mystery.

The mid-July sun streams in through my window, and I can already tell the day is going to be sticky and hot. I carefully set down Wes's shell. It still smells a little like the ocean—salty and fresh. The scent mixes with the strong odor of onions wafting through my bedroom door. Someone must be cooking downstairs.

I get dressed in a pair of jean shorts and a black T-shirt. They aren't the clothes that I would normally wear, but this new version of me—Lydia 2, as I've been thinking of her—doesn't care much about fashion. I feel a pang for the dresses and skirts that my great-aunt Mary loaned me in the forties, and for a moment I remember what it was like to get ready in her pink bedroom, rifling through her closet as she lay on the bed reading magazines and laughing.

I yank my dark red hair into a high ponytail, pulling tighter and tighter, until the pain makes my eyes water and the memory disappears.

My footsteps echo through the house as I walk down the stairs. My father is sitting in the living room, in his old armchair, drinking coffee. It's comforting to see him in a place I recognize, doing something he always used to do. "Hey Dad," I call softly.

He looks up from the paper he's reading. Even from across the room I can see his deep green eyes, the same color as my own.

"Oh, Lydia. Hi." He shakes his head a little, like he's surprised that I'm talking to him.

"What are you reading?" My voice sounds overly cheery.

He shrugs and stares down at the page in his hands. "An article."

There's a pause. I clear my throat. "Where's Mom?"

"Kitchen."

I twist my fingers together so hard they start to ache. The father I remember was easy to talk to, funny and kind. So different from this one. "Right. Are you going to eat with us? I'm sure Mom made tons of food. You know how she is. . . ." I laugh awkwardly.

"In a bit."

"Okay." I wait, but he doesn't say anything else. I leave the room.

The kitchen is filled with smoke. My mother stands at the stove wearing a linen pants suit, her sleek blond hair curling around her shoulders.

"Lydia, set the table, please."

I cough and wave my hand in front of my face. "Are you trying to burn the house down or something?"

My old mother would have laughed, but this new one turns icy-brown eyes on me and raises her eyebrow. I try not to flinch.

"Sorry," I mumble, and grab the plates out of the cupboard. I carefully set them down on the table.

Mom turns from the stove carrying a steaming pan. She has cut an onion and mushroom omelet into three thick pieces, and slides one of them onto my plate before she stops and gives me a look.

"Lydia." She sighs. "You did it again."

"What?"

"The plates."

I stare down at the china. It takes me a minute to realize what she means—I set the table for four instead of three.

But of course Grandpa's not here now.

"Sorry." I pick up one of the plates and set it on the counter.

Mom finishes serving the food. "Why do you keep doing that?"

"I don't know." I shrug as I take my seat at the table.

She drops the pan into the sink. It clatters against the other dishes, so loud that I jump and wonder if she broke something. "You've been acting different lately." Her voice is matter-of-fact, without the warmth I'm used to. She sits down at the table and stares at me. "What's going on with you?"

I glance at her with surprise; this is the first real question she's asked me in five weeks. "Nothing."

She tilts her head to the side. "Something's different."

"It's not. I'm the same."

"No. You're not." She picks up her fork and stabs the omelet on her plate. "You're . . . more sensitive. Forgetful. Do you feel all right? Is something going on at school?"

"It's the summer. School has been out for a month, remember?"

"Oh right." She looks flustered. "What about with Hannah? Or Grant?"

"They're fine. I'm fine." I force myself to smile at her.

"Everything's normal, Mom."

"See, that's what I mean."

"What?"

"Since when did you start calling me Mom?"

I frown. "What else would I call you?"

"You've been calling me Carol for the past three years. And you're never usually at home this much, or volunteering to help out at your father's store. What has gotten into you?"

Lydia 2 calls her mother Carol? I've been trying to learn her behavior, but I never expected this life to be so different from the one I left behind. Avoiding Mom's gaze, I reach up to push my bangs back from my forehead. But I freeze when I see her eyes narrow at the movement. Lydia 2 doesn't have bangs, and when I came back from the past it was something I had to quickly figure out how to explain.

"Nothing, sorry . . . Carol." But it feels so strange to say it that I cough and reach for the orange juice Mom put out earlier.

She scrapes her fork against her plate and meets my eyes. "You'll tell me if something is seriously wrong, right?"

"Um . . ." I am saved from answering when my father enters the room.

He sits down at the table without saying anything and starts to eat. My mother rolls her eyes at him and stands up abruptly. The action makes me smile—it's something my original mother would have done.

So is caring about what's going on with my life. Five weeks ago, when I first met this new Mom, I never would have thought she'd ask me how I'm doing. Maybe I underestimated her. Or maybe I'm starting to rub off on her.

It's a nice thought, that some of the old me is influencing this new life. But it also fills me with a sharp fear. I set my fork down and push my chair back.

"I have to go. I'll be late meeting Hannah."

"You're not done eating yet," Mom says.

"I'm not hungry. And we're going to the diner anyway."

"You'll be at the store later, though, right?" Dad doesn't look up from his plate.

"Yeah."

"There's some inventory to do. I left it on the desk in the back room."

"I'll get it done." I reach the door but stop and turn to face them. Mom is at the sink, her back to me.

Dad never stops eating. He looks older than he used to: there's gray hair at his temples and his mouth is framed by deep grooves when he frowns.

I hesitate. "Are we eating together tonight?"

Mom shakes her head without turning around. "I have a meeting."

The tiny bit of intimacy we just shared already feels like a distant memory. "See you both later then."

I fly out of the room and toward the front of the house. Wes was right—I stayed exactly the same after I traveled through the time machine, but I returned to a world I barely recognize. My family and friends expect me to be Lydia 2, with her thoughts and memories, and from the minute I arrived back in 2012 I've been trying to learn how to become this new version of myself.

It turns out that I'm the biggest mystery of all.

The red Toyota is already outside, idling on the curb near the front of my house. I rush down the driveway and yank open the passenger-side door.

"Whoa, what the hell, Lydia? Are you that excited to eat greasy fries?" Hannah asks as I slide into the battered leather seat.

"I just needed out." I lean back and stare at the only home I've ever known. It has lost all of the coziness I'm used to. The gray siding is drab, and the windows are shadowed. Even the gutters look unfriendly, overflowing with leaves. My dad would never have let it get like that.

Without thinking, I reach up to touch the pocket watch Wes gave me.

"Yeah, I don't blame you." Hannah pulls away from the curb and heads into downtown Montauk. "We could freeze ice on your mom's ass."

"This is true." But I think of that moment at the table. "She did just ask me a question about my life. Maybe she's starting to change."

"What kind of question?" Hannah sounds suspicious.

"Something about you and Grant," I say vaguely, not wanting to draw attention to my mother thinking I'm a different person lately—which I am. But Hannah is the only one in my life who hasn't changed much, and I can be myself around her in a way I can't with anyone else.

"Well, I'm shocked. She isn't exactly in the running for Mother of the Year."

"Not lately anyway." I look out the windshield as we drive around Fort Pond. The sunlight reflects off the water, and I can see the main drag of Montauk up ahead; the diner we're headed for is right across the town green.

"So, is lover boy coming to meet us for eggs?"

I bite my bottom lip. "I guess so."

"You know, he's a Cancer, you're an Aries, it's not going to—"

"I already know what you think," I snap. "I get it."

"Sheesh." Hannah sighs loudly. "Fine. New topic."

The downtown area is packed with tourists. Hannah manages to find a parking spot on a side street, where we're facing the beach. Even though it's not yet noon, people cover every inch of sand. Striped umbrellas, volleyball nets, and lifeguard towers block our view of the water.

As soon as I open the car door, I smell the ocean and feel the heat of the sun beating down on my head. Sweat instantly gathers at my temples.

"Ugh, it's like a million degrees today." Hannah lifts up her straight black hair and fans her neck. "Let's get to air-conditioning before I die out here."

"You're so dramatic." A family passes us: two little kids run for the ocean while their parents lag behind, carrying coolers and towels and already looking disgruntled.

Hannah glances over at me. "*I'm* the dramatic one? Says the girl who believes in crazy government conspiracies! That's rich, Lyd."

I frown. "Can you just let it go?"

She holds her hands up. "You're the one who's always going off about time travel and aliens and scientists who fake their own death."

"Whatever," I mumble. "A lot of people around here believe in that stuff."

"It doesn't make it any less crazy."

At the look on my face, she grabs my elbow. "Oh come on, I'm starving." She tugs me toward the diner. "I promise not to tease you about wormholes anymore, okay?"

The diner is blasting cool air, and the shock of it causes goose bumps to rise on my skin. Hannah, who hasn't let go of my arm, pulls me to our favorite table. The diner has a fifties feel to it, with red vinyl booths and a long, shiny, silver counter. The waitress comes by and I order a chocolate milk shake. Hannah gets coffee, black.

"What time do you have to go to work?" Hannah picks up the menu and glances at it more out of habit than necessity—we both have it memorized at this point.

"Noon."

The waitress sets two waters down in front of us. I grab a straw and pull off the wrapper, fiddling with the fragile paper.

"I don't know why you don't just quit. You hate working there."

"Yeah, but my dad needs me. We've been slammed lately. People watch all those home improvement shows and think they can do it themselves."

Hannah crosses her arms over the loose brown tank dress she's wearing. Even in this time line she dresses like a hippie. She claims that it's an ironic homage to her free-spirit parents—her mom owns a record shop outside of town and her father is an experimental artist from Japan—but I think her family has affected her more than she lets on. Despite being insanely cynical, she does have a persistent superstitious streak.

Like her insistance that horoscopes actually mean something.

Signs. Aries. Leo. I instantly picture Wes, tall and lean, dark-haired and dark-eyed, standing by an army jeep, the black water of the ocean moving behind him. I told him Leos are supposed to be strong and protective, and he told me about being a recruit in the Montauk Project. I think that's why he left me, in the end, because he knew they wouldn't let him go and he wanted to keep me safe.

But who's keeping him safe?

"You know what you need, Lydia?" Hannah asks. I pull myself out of my Wes-induced fog and look at her.

"What?"

"A hobby. And not that Camp Hero stuff you're always talking about. You should go out for the cheerleading squad next year or something."

"The cheerleading squad? But then you'd never speak to me again."

She purses her lips. "You're right. Plus you're not peppy enough. Hmm . . ." She taps her finger on the table, one-two, one-two. A steady beat. "How about the literary mag? No wait, I would have to make so much fun of you if you started writing poetry about all your teenage angst."

The waitress comes back with our drinks and takes our order. I sip on the milk shake, holding the cold glass in my fingers, grateful that I have something to do with my hands. I don't often feel uncomfortable around Hannah, but I don't often have to lie to her either.

Because I can't tell her the truth—that I do have a hobby. Journalism. Or, I used to have it. But Lydia 2 is not interested in things like the school newspaper and therefore has time to work in her father's store all summer.

No, Lydia 2 has other things to focus on.

"Don't look now," Hannah says, "but your boyfriend is coming."

I hear someone walk into the diner, and I turn my head. A tall black-haired boy is walking toward us with a wide grin on his face.

"Hey Grant!" Hannah calls out.

I feel my heart start to race.

"Hey Hannah," he says as soon as he's close enough to us. "Lydia."

And then he's there, right in front of me. He leans forward, closer and closer, and I brace myself against the metal tabletop. My eyes are open and staring, and I notice that Grant's cheek is pale and freckled this close up. I feel his lips touch mine softly.

He pulls away. "Hey, you."

I press my lips together hard as he bends again, this time to sit next to me in our small booth. Our arms, our sides are touching. He's talking, though I don't hear what he's saying.

This is one part of my new life I'm having a hard time adjusting to.

Grant Henderson, the boy I grew up next door to, a boy I never thought I could fall in love with, is my boyfriend.

CHAPTER 2

I have been thinking a lot about fate lately. My own. My grandfather's. Wes's. How much do I really understand fate? Grandpa disappeared in 1989 in this time line. But that wasn't always his fate. Just like it wasn't always Dean's fate to get lost in time, probably to 1920, where he'll be trapped forever. I changed those things by traveling back to 1944.

And now I'm sitting in a booth with Grant's arm around me.

I feel something nudge my side and I look up. Both Hannah and Grant are staring at me, clearly waiting for a response.

"What?" I ask. "Sorry, I spaced out."

Grant laughs softly and rubs his hand against my shoulder. "You've been doing that a lot lately."

I lean forward until I can't feel his touch anymore. "I have stuff on my mind."

"Is it the Montauk Project again? I think we should go out there today. I was reading through that book you gave me a while ago, the one on alternating currents. I think—"

He's cut off by Hannah, who holds up both hands and starts waving them back and forth. "No! No way. Absolutely no crazy government conspiracy crap today. I get that it's your weird couple thing, or whatever, but I'm trying to enjoy a nice, calm breakfast without any talk of repta . . . repto . . ."

"Reptoids," I finish quietly. "They're called reptoids."

"Right. Reptoids." Hannah's voice is getting louder. The other diners start to look over. "I don't care that the government supposedly tapped into wormholes and contacted secret alien species that look like snake-human hybrids. I don't care about Nikola Tesla faking his own death. I. Do. Not. Care." She sits back in her seat and takes a deep breath.

Grant and I both stare at her.

She rolls her eyes. "Don't look at me like I'm crazy— you're the ones who believe in aliens."

"I don't believe in aliens," I say.

Grant turns to me, one dark eyebrow raised. "You've never said that before. I thought you were a 'true believer.'"

"I am . . . I just . . . don't necessarily think aliens are part of it." And I don't, not since Wes assured me they're fiction, along with the theory that Tesla faked his own death. It was Dr. Faust who invented the time machine, using Tesla's research on rotating magnetic fields.

"Lydia." Grant sounds shocked. "You've always believed in reptoids. When you were six you claimed you *saw* one on the beach out by Hero."

I shrug, not sure what to say. It's a familiar feeling these days.

My grandfather was always convinced the Montauk Project had something to do with his father's disappearance. In this time line, Lydia 2 has taken his place. *She's* the one who has always been obsessed with the Project, certain that they were behind my grandfather's disappearance in 1989.

Lydia 2 never knew her grandfather the way I did. To her, he was just a family legend, shrouded in mystery. Since I've been back, I have only picked through a few of the papers and notebooks on her desk. It was enough to know that Lydia 2 had found my grandfather's journals, and through them had learned about the Montauk Project. I can only assume that my father wouldn't talk about it, and so she set out to find what information she could on her own, obsessed with the thought of what her family would be like if my grandfather had never disappeared.

It's strange how history repeats itself, even across a new version of time.

"Well, if you're starting to get sick of all this stuff, I completely and totally approve," Hannah tells me.

I nod. I can feel Grant watching me, and I glance at him

from the corner of my eye. His dark hair falls over his forehead in a messy wave, and he's wearing a T-shirt that says IRONY in big black letters.

"I can't believe I'm even hearing this," he says softly. "We've always believed that the Montauk Project was real. It's why we . . ." He waves his hand in the air between us.

"I know, I'm just . . ." I turn away, concentrating on the framed records hanging on the wall above our heads. As far as I can tell, Lydia 2 devoted almost all of her time to the Montauk Project—and to Grant by association.

The whole thing suddenly makes me irrationally angry. I didn't pick Grant, but here I am, forced to pretend I'm in love with him.

And his shirt is stupid anyway.

"Look, I need to get to work." I lean over, hoping he'll take the hint and move out of the booth. He doesn't.

"You don't have to be in for an hour," he says. He's starting to look less hurt and more worried. "Your food hasn't even come yet. What's going on with you?"

"I'm not hungry anymore. You should eat it." My words are clipped and short.

"Lydia, come on." Hannah's eyes are wide with concern. "Stay."

"I'm sorry." I sigh. "I'm fine . . . just tired, I guess. I'll call you both later, okay?"

"All right. If you're sure nothing's wrong." Grant stands up and holds out his hand. I reluctantly let him pull me up and out of the booth. "See you soon." I jerk to the side before his mouth can land on mine. His lips graze my cheek.

"Bye." I lift my hand up at Hannah, and then rush toward the door. It opens as I reach it, and Shannon Perkins and a few other cheerleaders from school stream into the diner. They are talking and laughing, but Shannon meets my eye as she pushes past me.

"Excuse me," she says quickly.

I smile automatically. "Shannon, hi! I haven't seen you all summer."

She gives me an odd look, and the rest of her friends stop and stare at us. "Oh. Lydia. Hi."

At her tone, I freeze. Of course, Lydia 2 and Shannon weren't childhood friends, and now I look like a complete ass. "Sorry, I'll just be . . ." I reach around one of the girls and fumble for the door handle. Someone giggles, a high, mocking sound. I feel Hannah and Grant staring at my back, wondering how I could possibly think I'm friends with a group of cheerleaders. My face is hot as I exit the diner.

I'm not doing a very good job of being myself today.

Halfway down the sidewalk, I stop and take a deep breath. I shouldn't have run away like that, but I don't *want* to be Lydia 2 anymore. I miss being myself. I miss my parents, and journalism, and even my old organized bedroom.

But most of all, I miss my grandfather.

The most logical step is to stop trying to be someone I'm not. To give up on Lydia 2 and re-create my old life as best I can, starting with dumping Grant. I could join the newspaper again and try to build a new relationship with my parents. I'd never get my grandfather back, but I might be able to reclaim some of the life I remember.

Only I can't.

Because I'm too scared.

The old me would have barged into this new life, deter-mined to find out what happened to my grandfather and to fix it. But something changed in me after I watched Dean get sucked into the time machine. After I saw a bullet tear through Wes's shoulder, his blood dripping to the white floor.

The last time I tampered with the past, I changed—and lost—so much. What if changing something in this new time line affects the future in some horrible, unknowable way?

But this isn't working. I have been trying so hard to neatly slot into Lydia 2's life: re-creating her relationship with my parents, not disrupting things with Grant, trying to come to terms with Wes being gone. Today proves that it's not enough. Even my absent mother is noticing that I've changed. I can't completely hide who I am.

Maybe it's time to let go of that fear. To start reclaiming my old life again, at least a little bit.

———

A bell dings as the door to my father's hardware store opens.

I turn toward the sound. "Can I help you?"

A man stands in the doorway. The afternoon sun falls down on him from the front windows, making his honey-colored skin look like it's glowing.

"Lydia Bentley."

I straighten. "Do I know you?"

He smiles at my suspicious tone and starts to come closer. The shop is small and cluttered, so he has to walk carefully. Shovels hang on the walls and piles of rakes are stacked in the corner like forks nestled in a silverware drawer. The man skirts a bag of fertilizer and a large clay pot as he approaches the counter. I slowly shut the magazine I've been reading.

"I was just getting ready to close." The shop is empty except for the two of us. The man looks harmless, but how does he know my name?

I slowly reach for the phone that my dad keeps tucked under the counter.

"It's okay. We know each other."

I look him over. He's of medium height, with short dark hair, thick eyebrows, and a wide nose. I'd guess he's in his midthirties. "I'm sorry, but I've never seen you before."

At my words, he tilts his head, assessing me. His smile fades. "You really don't know who I am, do you?"

I rest my hand on the cool plastic of the portable phone, but I don't pick it up. Not yet. "Should I?"

He nods. "I'm Jonathan. . . . But you know me as Resister."

"Resister?"

"From the boards." At my blank stare, he continues to explain. "Message boards. The Montauk Conspiracy message boards?"

"What did you just say?" My hand clenches, curling tightly around the phone.

"You haven't been on in a while, but we did plan to meet today . . . so here I am."

"You're a conspiracy theorist. And you came here to meet Lydia—I mean me," I repeat.

He gives me a calculating look. "You're Montauk17, right? We've been talking for months. You said you had some new information on why your grandfather disappeared. And I have some new information too. On . . ." He leans in closer. "On the rebellion."

"What rebellion?" I ask, despite myself. I had no idea that Lydia 2 was going on message boards to talk about the Montauk Project, though it makes sense that she would try to connect with other conspiracy theorists. I wonder how much information she actually uncovered.

I quickly look at the exposed front windows of the shop. If this man is too close to the truth, the Project might be watching him.

"I think it's only a matter of time before we'll be organized." His voice drops. "That's just the beginning. I have a list of everyone they've taken, Lydia. You know that. I've been using it to find them."

I know I should make him leave, but the curiosity is too great. "Everyone they're taken. Do you mean . . . ?"

His brown eyes are wide, making him look a little unhinged as he says, "Recruits."

I jerk back. "Recruits? You know how to find a recruit?"

"Not yet. But I've been tracking someone. I'm close to making contact."

Can he really find a recruit? Could he find Wes? And then his words fully sink in. At best, this man is a conspiracy nut who stumbled into something he doesn't understand—because there's no way he'd be able to make contact with a recruit. They'd kill him first. At worst, he's working with the Project and was sent here because Lydia 2 was getting too close to the truth. Or maybe he's here for me. Maybe they've finally realized *I* was involved in time line changes in 1944. He could be trying to feel me out, to discover how much information I have before he kills me.

"You don't know what you're talking about," I snap, trying to ignore how fast my heart is beating.

His expressive eyebrows almost meet in the middle of his forehead as he frowns. "I do. Trust me."

"I have no reason to trust you." I take a step back and press the phone into my chest. It makes a sharp noise as it collides with Wes's watch. "You need to leave now."

"Lydia . . ." He moves closer to me, and I flinch away from him. "I need your help."

"If you don't leave I'm calling the police."

He grits his teeth together and holds up both hands. "Okay. Okay. I'm leaving." He starts to back away. I watch him go, holding my breath. The door pings again when he opens it, but he pauses before exiting the shop.

"I messed this up. I hadn't realized . . ." He trails off. "I have a feeling we'll meet again, Lydia." And then he's gone.

I run around the counter, not stopping until I reach the door. With a quick flick of my wrist I lock it and then flip the Closed sign until it's facing the street. I back away from the front windows, frantically scanning the sidewalk, but the man has already disappeared.

The backs of my calves hit a flowerpot and I sink down onto the ground, clutching my knees. The Montauk Project hasn't found me. He was just another crazy conspiracy theorist. It's okay. It's going to be okay.

Even though I repeat the words over and over, I can't seem to make myself believe them.

Later that night, I stand over my desk. I may have briefly glanced at Lydia 2's files—enough to know that she was looking into my grandfather's disappearance—but I've mostly been avoiding this part of her life since I came back to 2012.

Meeting that man today proves that I can't let myself stay in the dark any longer. It's too dangerous. I need to know everything Lydia 2 knows if I'm going to be safe.

I pull out my desk chair and sit down. The surface of the desk is covered with books, papers, and Lydia 2's laptop. There is also a stack of notebooks in the corner—my grandfather's journals. I hesitate for a second, then force myself to pick one up. The cover is dated April 1989. I open the cheap black notebook to a page in the middle. The paper is soft with age and almost falling out of its binding. The words I find are barely legible, written with pencil, faded and sloppy. Not that they make much sense anyway. As far as I can tell, it's just a random collection of letters and numbers, strung together: $SO4N2H11C9OC9H11N2O4S$. The pattern keeps repeating, but I have no idea what it could mean. I put it aside.

The next journal is dated 1985. I read the first entry, written in my grandfather's broad, slanting script:

Today, I took Jake to look at cars. He's already 16. Almost a man. Sometimes it seems like yesterday when he was born. I told him about my father on the way over to the dealership. He wasn't interested, of course, but he's a teenager, consumed by other things.

Lately, I am finding it harder and harder to think about anything other than my own father's disappearance. I pore over his journal, rereading every line, wondering what took him from us. I've been hearing rumors about what happens out at Camp Hero. They say it's shut down, but there are strange flashes of light and disappearances that can't be explained. Disappearances like my father's. What's happening out there?

I slam the notebook shut and it shakes in my hands. In the original time line, Grandpa didn't become obsessed with the Montauk Project until I was a little girl, after his wife died and he found his father's journal hidden underneath a floorboard. But in this time line he had already found it by the 1980s. Was it Dean's journal that set him down this path so early?

I rest my fingers on the worn black cover. What happened between 1985 and 1989 to reduce my grandfather to that strange repetition of letters and numbers?

It takes me a few hours to flip through the rest of the notebooks. Grandpa was coherent until about 1987, though he had already discovered the Montauk Project and was beginning to contact other conspiracy theorists. But there's a gap in his writing between 1987 and 1989. Then, the last journal reads like gibberish.

After going back in time to 1944, I learned not to discount my grandfather's ideas so quickly. He was right about the Montauk Project and what happened to Dean. But he was also never this unintelligible. Could $SO4N2H11C9O-C9H11N2O4S$ actually mean something? Is the pattern important?

I toss the journals aside and contemplate the mess on Lydia 2's desk. She was researching his disappearance; more information has to be here somewhere.

I find what I'm looking for in a folder on her laptop—it's called the Project and has pictures of Camp Hero mixed with Word files documenting what Lydia 2 knew. I open a few of the files, but they're mostly the same old theories my grandfather used to tell me over and over: reptoids and Tesla and wormholes. I finally discover a file titled "Peter Bentley.doc." It is a complete breakdown in outline form of my grandfather's life, from when he was born, in 1937, to when he disappeared, on August 14, 1989.

My grandfather's obsession with his father was driven by love and a desire to find out why his family was torn apart when he was a child. But Lydia 2 never loved my grandfather, and the file in front of me reads like an impersonal list of facts.

I skim through the document, a part of me wondering why Lydia 2 would care so much about solving the mystery of a man she never even knew. But then I think of how distant her parents are, and must have always been. At the core, Lydia 2 and I are still the same person, with a driving desire to discover the truth. With a loving family, I channeled that energy into journalism. Without that, Lydia 2 became consumed with the mystery that might explain why her family was so fractured.

I vaguely note the dates my grandfather graduated high school, married my grandmother, and opened his hardware store. But an entry near the bottom of the page makes me stop. "Oh my God," I breathe.

On July 5, 1989, my grandfather was committed to Bellevue Psychiatric Hospital. He would remain there until his disappearance.

Did he really go insane in this time line, finally pushed to the edge by his obsession with the Montauk Project? Or, like before, was everyone simply writing him off as crazy, unwilling to see the truth in his theories?

I scroll back up the page and read more carefully. Apparently my grandmother was fed up with his obsession over the Project and kicked him out in 1988. He moved into an apartment in New York City shortly after, forcing my father to drop out of college to run Bentley's Hardware. Dad was also the one who committed Grandpa to Bellevue in 1989.

"Well, that explains why my dad is so different in this time line," I mutter under my breath as I click through the file.

According to Lydia 2's document, that final afternoon, a nurse went to check on Grandpa and he wasn't in his room. They did a sweep of the hospital, but he had vanished. No one ever saw him again.

The staff at Bellevue assumed that he somehow snuck out of the hospital and later died on the streets of New York. But Lydia 2 didn't believe it, convinced that the Montauk Project had something to do with his disappearance.

Was she right? Was the Project trying to silence my grandfather for some reason?

I finish reading and sit back, staring at the screen until it starts to get blurry. My grandfather, the man who helped raise me, ended up in a mental institution. And it's my fault—if I hadn't changed something in the past, none of this would have happened. This was exactly why I didn't want to look into Lydia 2's information on the Montauk Project; I was scared of what I might find.

I used to think it was always better to know the truth. But I didn't know how frustrating it would feel when there's nothing you can do to make things right again.

I squeeze my hands into fists. All I want to do is go to sleep and forget about what I just learned. But the man's words from earlier come back to me: *"The Montauk Conspiracy message boards."* Lydia 2 wasn't just investigating Grandpa; she was also involved with this Resister person. But does he really know how to find a recruit, or is he secretly working for the Project? Are they monitoring me, even now?

I hesitate for a minute, my fingers hovering over the keyboard. Outside it is getting darker, but I haven't turned on any lamps and the computer is the only bright spot in the room. It puts out an artificial glow that reminds me of the fluorescent lights down in the Facility at Camp Hero. I shiver as I remember running through those white corridors, desperately searching for a way out.

If the Project suspected me, they wouldn't be sending some conspiracy theorist into my father's shop to question me. I would already be dead.

Which means the Resister was telling the truth. I don't know if he's really onto something, but if I can find the message board he was talking about then I might be able to figure out what he meant by "the rebellion."

I close the file on Grandpa and open Safari. Lydia 2 has several saved bookmarks, and I find one called "MP Boards." A white log-in screen pops up. I type in Lydia's handle: Montauk17. But I pause when it asks for a password.

I try *Reptoids.* Nothing. *Tesla. Grant. LydiaBentley.* None of it works. Finally I type in my grandfather's name: *Peter-Bentley.* The screen disappears, and is replaced by a standard forum template with a black background and bright green lettering. I skim through some of the message-board subject headings. One is labeled *Tesla Still Alive!* Another reads *Visiting Camp Hero.*

A small box pops up on the screen in front of me. *Tgirl123 is inviting you to a private chat.* I click on the link provided, and a new page loads.

Tgirl123: Heyya. Where the hell you been?

I slowly type out a response.

Montauk17: Sorry. Been busy. Anything new?

Tgirl123: Resister's all over the private chats. He's close.

Montauk17: To what?

Tgirl123: Are you kidding? The rebellion!

I sit up straighter. How is this safe to talk about here? With nothing to lose, I ask her.

Tgirl123: Girl, please. You know Resister is all over that shit. He's hidden this board from everyone! Not even the MP could find it.

So not only is the Resister organizing against the Project, but he knows enough about computers to hide an entire internet community from their eyes?

Montauk17: What's the next step?

Tgirl123: Says there's a recruit he's close to cracking. He's getting a spy in the Project. Once we know how they work we can start the takedown.

Montauk17: How do we do that?

Tgirl123: It's all in the time machine! We're making our own!

These conspiracy theorists must be trying to get to a recruit in order to access Dr. Faust's prototype for the time machine. Or Tesla's machine, as Wes called it—the TM.

But how do they know about the recruits? I never even knew that information, not until Wes told me about how they kidnapped him.

Before I can ask, the words *Gotta go. Later.* appear on the screen.

Tgirl123 signs out, and I'm in this private chat room by myself. I close it and search through a few of the main forums, but no one is talking about anything I haven't heard before. There's nothing on the rebellion, and I wonder if maybe this is a private idea, shared only among a few select people.

I read through back entries until my eyes hurt, but there's nothing to connect my grandfather to the Montauk Project. And no Resister in sight.

Why does it seem like no matter what I do, I only create

more questions, more mysteries?

Frustrated, I slam the laptop shut and shove it across the cluttered desk. It skids a few inches on the piles of paper and crashes into Wes's leaf. I reach out, but it's too late: the dried leaf is crushed into small pieces.

I stand up so quickly my desk chair falls to the floor.

This is so pointless. I don't even know that the leaf was from Wes. Anyone could have left those things on the windowsill. It was probably Grant, trying to be romantic. Or a squirrel.

I spin around and fall face-first onto my bed.

Anything could have happened to Wes since I last saw him in the time-machine room, blood leaking out of his shoulder. His life is always in danger, with the constant fear that if he doesn't die from the effects of the time machine, he'll die on a mission he's forced to go on. The odds he'd reach out to me, with the Project watching his every move, are slim. Would he take that risk just to leave me some trinkets? Or am I so desperate for some sign of him that I've been convincing myself he's thinking of me at all?

Is he even still alive?

Please let him still be alive.

If only I could see him one more time, I might not feel so alone.

I reach under my pillow and pull out a neatly folded piece of paper. I carefully smooth it out and stare down at a photocopy of an old wedding announcement.

Jacob and Harriet Bentley have the pleasure of announcing the marriage of their daughter, Mary Bentley, a local nurse, to former army sergeant Lucas Clarke. The two were wed this past Saturday, June 5, 1945, at the home of Dr. Bentley and his wife. They will retire to Mr. Clarke's family farm in White Plains, Georgia, to start their life together.

I rub my finger over the small black-and-white photo of Mary and Lucas that accompanies the article. She is in a simple white dress, her hair in curls, and she's beaming up at Lucas. He has his arm around her and is looking straight at the camera. Even in the faded ink I can see his crooked bottom teeth as he smiles.

As soon as I got back to 2012, I went to the local library and looked up information on the Bentleys. Aside from old case files of Dr. Bentley, this was the only thing I could find.

This picture was taken almost seventy years in the past, and yet it feels like yesterday I was at the USO dance, watching Mary and Lucas spin across a crowded floor. I was worried that I had screwed up their destinies too, by going back into the past. But even though Dean went missing, they still ended up together, and they look happy.

I clutch the paper in my hands. How can I feel so homesick when I'm technically home? Mary and Lucas are gone. I might still have Hannah, but I don't have my family. I don't have Wes. And my grandfather disappeared because I inadvertently changed his destiny.

There is no time or place that I belong to, not anymore.

I can't stop them; the tears come, burning my eyes and soaking the pillow beneath me. I try to keep quiet at first, but then I remember that these parents probably wouldn't care either way.

I've lost everything.

Sometime in the night, I jerk awake. I'm lying on my back, still in my jean shorts and loose T-shirt. My face feels puffy and raw, and the tears have dried into salty tracks that run down my cheeks.

My heart is pounding, though I'm not sure why. I reach up, my hand closing around the cool metal of Wes's pocket watch. I was dreaming. About being with Wes, and the woods in fall, red and orange leaves drifting all around us.

I feel strange, like something has changed without my knowledge. I sit up quickly. The moon is spilling silver light onto the edge of my bed. I glance around the room and gasp as one of the shadows near the window breaks away from the wall. I try to scream, but I'm frozen as it moves and reforms.

It is coming closer, and I clench my fingers in the bed-spread. A dark shape looms over me.

It is a person, I realize. A boy. And then the light from the moon slides across his face.

Wes.

CHAPTER 3

"It's you," I whisper.

"Lydia." His voice is hoarse. The sound of it breaks through the spell holding me still, and I rise onto my knees to face him.

"God, Wes. Where have you been? Are you okay? How's your shoulder? Have you been leaving those things on my windowsill?" The words spill out of me, an endless flood I can't stop.

"So many questions." He smiles a little, so that just the corners of his mouth tilt up. "You haven't changed."

The comment makes something open inside of me, something I hadn't realized was locked up tight. "I guess not."

He doesn't answer but steps closer. He moves with the

same careful deliberateness I remember. He's so familiar that it makes my chest hurt. I've been waiting to see his face for weeks, imagining his arms folded around me. But now that he's here, I'm not sure how to act. The last thing he did was send me away from him, telling me we couldn't be together.

As he gets closer, I see the weary look in his eyes. Something is wrong.

"What is it? Are you hurt?" I put my arm out but stop before I make contact, not sure if he'll welcome it.

"No." He lets the word hang there and steps closer. He's dressed in the black, slick-looking uniform that all the recruits wear.

My hand is still outstretched and Wes takes another step and suddenly I'm touching him. I close my eyes as my fingertips graze his rib cage.

"You kept it."

I look up. He's staring down at the watch that's resting against my chest.

"Of course I did."

He leans in further and my hand flattens against his stomach. This time he's the one who closes his eyes.

The moon is bright enough for me to see his face clearly. His nose has a slight bump at the bridge where I know he's broken it. His cheekbones are sharp, his jaw even more pronounced. I wonder if he's lost weight since I saw him last.

His eyelids slowly open and his black eyes lock onto

mine. "I shouldn't be here."

"Don't go." I try to grip the fabric of his shirt, but it slips out of my hand. I pull back, staring at the dark liquid covering my palm.

"Are you bleeding?"

"It's not mine."

I reach for him with both hands, but he lightly takes hold of my wrists.

"The last time I saw you, you were covered in blood. It was falling onto the floor." My voice cracks on the words.

"It's not mine. I'm fine. It's . . ." He looks away.

"Your arm. What happened?"

He keeps his grip on my wrists, connecting us even as he holds me apart from him.

"It was nothing. A flesh wound. It healed in a few days." He shrugs, and I relax a little at the easy way he moves his shoulder. "The TM screwed up; the machines in 1944 are too unpredictable. I got back a day before you were scheduled to come through, and I fixed myself up before anyone could notice. They never even knew I followed you through time."

"Wes." I shift closer to him until our hands are trapped between us. "Why are you here? No, wait," I say quickly. "I don't care what the reason is. I'm just happy to see you."

He drops my wrists and reaches up to cup my face. His hands are warm on my cheeks. "I didn't think I'd ever see you again." His voice is soft, a whisper.

"Me neither." I lift my hands and place them over his. The pose reminds me of the first time we kissed, pressed against a tree in 1944. "The shell. The flower. The leaf. Did you leave them for me?"

He leans forward until our foreheads touch. I can smell him now, and I take in breath like I'm trying not to drown.

I feel him nod against me. "It was stupid, I know. . . ."

I smile at the thought of him sneaking into my room at night while I slept. He didn't forget me. He didn't leave me here alone.

"It wasn't stupid," I say. "I needed to know you were here in some way."

"I was. *I am.*" The second he says the words, his arms stiffen and he lifts his head. "No, no, I shouldn't have said that. Lydia, I came here to tell you something. You have to forget me. You have to forget about all of it." He steps back, away from me.

"Wes." I put my arms out again, but he turns toward the window. "I don't understand. You've been leaving me those . . . gifts, and then you appear in my bedroom in the middle of the night to tell me that we can't be together? It doesn't make sense."

He bends his head and I watch as he runs his fingers through his black hair. It has grown longer since I last saw him; it curls around the back of his neck now. "I know. I know."

"What's wrong? What happened?"

"Nothing." He turns quickly to face me. "Lydia, just promise me that you'll forget about the Montauk Project. And about me."

I stare at him for a moment. His eyes are dark, unwavering, and I know he's serious. He thinks I can just forget about him?

"No." I shake my head. "I've tried to be this new Lydia. But I can't, Wes. It's not working. I can't forget myself, and I certainly can't forget you."

"You have to." He steps forward and his hands close around my upper arms.

"Why are you saying this?"

"Lydia." He squeezes me so hard I wince. At my expression, he lets go immediately. "They know," he says quietly.

"Who knows?"

"The Project. They know the time line is different. They had been monitoring this election in the past, and it changed. Now they're investigating the rift."

My fingers twist in the soft material of my T-shirt. All of a sudden I can't get enough air. "Do they know about me? Are they coming here?"

"Not yet." His voice, his face are blank. "One of the recruits who was in nineteen eighty-nine reported that a change happened in New York City." At my questioning look he explains, "A city council election has a different outcome. One that isn't . . . favorable for the Project. The information traveled to two thousand twelve. I've been ordered to investigate what it means. They're sending me to the past tomorrow."

An election changed. Was it because of something that I did in 1944? "Can they connect that to me?" I ask. "To us?"

"Not yet."

"It might have nothing to do with us. Recruits are all over history, changing the past. Maybe this recruit just screwed up." But the date—1989—is the same year my grandfather disappeared. Could it be connected?

Before I can tell Wes this, I hear him say, "It doesn't matter. I'll keep them away from you no matter what." I glance up. He's standing over me, his hands tight at his sides. "You'll be safe. But you have to protect yourself."

"What do you mean?"

Wes's eyes dart toward my cluttered desk. "You can't have any more connection with the Montauk Project. Burn everything and forget about it. Live your life here."

I press my lips together, afraid that I'm about to cry. "I'm trying, Wes, but I don't think I can do it. My grandfather is gone. My parents . . . everything is different. I miss you."

We stare at each other silently. Wes is the first one to look away. "Lydia," he whispers. "I watched a girl kill herself today." I make a small noise, but he keeps going. "One of the recruits took her gun and . . . right in front of me. Close enough that her blood soaked through my shirt. It's on my skin." He pauses. "She was the one who told them about the rift in time. They were investigating her, she . . ."

I climb out of the bed and lean into him, my cheek pressed against his shirt, his chest. I can feel the blood, sticky and cold, but I don't care. Wes, who not too long ago could barely smile at me, is too emotional to finish telling me what happened. His arms close around me and we stay there for a while, holding each other.

"I'm so sorry, Wes." I whisper the words into his chest.

"I keep thinking that it could be you. That I'll be washing your blood off me." He says it so quietly I almost don't hear him.

"It won't."

"This is what they do. They kill everyone around them. And when we survive, it's not really living. She's not the first recruit to take her own life, and I doubt she'll be the last."

I pull back to look up into his face. "Who was she?"

"They called her Seventeen. I don't know what her real name was. Maybe she didn't even remember anymore."

Wes is known in the Facility as Eleven. Now that Seventeen is dead, a newly trained recruit will take her place. And on and on the cycle goes. I don't know how many Elevens there have been before Wes. I'm too scared to ask.

"Was she a new recruit?"

Wes is in shadow, his expression hidden from me. "No. She wasn't. She was almost nineteen."

"Isn't that when you get too old to travel through the machine?"

"Sometimes." He abruptly lets go of me and walks to the

window. He peers out at the night sky. The stars are tiny dots of light above the black, hunched shapes of the trees.

"She killed herself during a patrol of the woods around Hero. I was with her. They told me to keep an eye on her, to make sure she wasn't lying about the election. After she . . . I hid her body. And I walked here. I had to see you, to warn you . . . I don't know. I wasn't thinking."

"I'm glad you came," I say softly.

He shifts slightly and I look at his profile in the moonlight—his sharp chin, the slight bump on his straight nose. The moon is behind him, the light gliding through his hair like some misplaced halo. "I have to go bury her."

"Will you tell them what she did?"

"Not yet. I don't want them to find her. They . . . do experiments on us."

Horror uncurls in my chest. I feel my mouth fall open. "They experiment on your bodies after you die?"

Wes keeps his face turned away from mine. "They want to study the effects of the TM on a deceased recruit. I didn't know Seventeen, not really, but I wouldn't let that happen to anyone. Not if I can help it." He is quiet for a moment. "I should go."

No.

He twists his head until our eyes meet.

I feel my whole body shudder as I see the blank resolve on his face. "Wes . . . don't."

"Good-bye, Lydia."

I rush forward, but I can't move quickly enough. He ducks down and out of the window. By the time I reach where he stood, he has already disappeared into the deep shadows near the side of the house.

"Come back," I whisper into the night.

But there's no answer.

I sink down on my bed in the dark. Wes is gone, this time for good. There will be no more shells on my windowsill. This is my life now—a mother and father I don't know, a boyfriend I didn't choose. No Grandfather. No Wes.

I can't lose him. *I won't.*

The thought forces me up. As if moving through deep water, I step toward the closet and pull out black sweats. I get dressed slowly, wondering if I'm dreaming, if Wes being here was just a figment of my imagination. But I can still feel the traces of blood on my hands.

It was real. I have a chance.

My house is silent this late at night. I wash my hands in the upstairs bathroom, and then tiptoe down the long hallway. The door to my parents' room is firmly shut, and I press my cheek to the cool wood. I think I hear them breathing inside, but it's probably just the sound of my heartbeat pulsing in my ears. "Good-bye," I whisper, not knowing when I'll see them again. If I ever will.

There is only a half moon tonight, but I don't need the light. I know where I'm going. I walk down the driveway, feet crunching on the loose gravel. I don't bother to be quiet, not yet.

It is a long walk in the darkness, and my sneakers make a steady, constant rhythm on the pavement. After a while, time starts to lose meaning and I can't tell if I've been out here for minutes or hours. It reminds me of hiding in the back of Lucas's truck as he drove us to Camp Hero. I was so afraid of what I was walking into, but there was something lulling, calming, about crouching in total blackness in a place that seemed to exist outside of time.

That was the night Mary caught me sneaking back into the Bentleys' house and I told her I was meeting Wes because I was in love with him. I wasn't, not then, but I'm glad that I didn't completely lie to her. Because here I am, running away to be with him.

I walk through downtown Montauk. Only when I reach the highway do I veer to the right, up over the dunes and out of sight of any passing cars. I'm the only person on the long stretch of beach, and all I can hear is the shuffling of my feet on the wet sand and the waves breaking hard against the shore. The whole world has been reduced to black and white—the dark spread of the water and the moon shining silver and gray above it all.

It is late and getting later. I move more quickly.

Before the forest starts, I climb off of the beach and into the trees. I'm on the west side of the park, and though I don't know exactly where Wes is, I have a pretty good idea. He said he needed to take care of the body and there are only so many places that are far enough away from the Montauk Project's Facility.

I scan the woods as I walk, listening for unfamiliar sounds. The smell of the ocean fades, overwhelmed by the scent of fresh dirt and green, growing things. There is a fence up ahead, but long ago someone ripped a hole in the chain link, probably a conspiracy theorist out looking for clues. I duck through the small space, wincing as the metal bites into my skin.

The southwestern side of Camp Hero is the most deserted part. I walk slowly through the woods, remembering the countless times I came here with my grandfather. The memories leave me feeling empty. I was never receptive to Grandpa's theories, but at least in this time line he had me to confide in. How lonely it must be to quietly lose yourself in your own mind.

It is darker in the dense forest, with almost no moonlight shining through the heavy canopy of leaves overhead. Knotted branches of trees reach out for me as I pass. The last time I visited Camp Hero at night, I was sneaking into the Facility, praying that I could warn Dean before he disappeared. But I failed then.

I can't fail now.

Wes and Seventeen were on patrol, so there probably aren't any other recruits out here—but I can't be too careful. I know what happens in these woods. I move more cautiously through the trees and underbrush. But it's too dark to see the ground clearly, and I keep tripping over roots and large rocks.

My toe collides with a sharp stick and I stumble. I hiss under my breath and then freeze as I hear something rustle the leaves.

I wait, perfectly still, but there's no other sound. I straighten and take another step.

"You're making too much noise."

The whisper comes from my left and I spin toward it to see Wes standing there, silhouetted in the trees.

"I'm trying to be quiet."

He comes closer. The night creates hard planes on his face, and even in the dark I can tell that he's scowling. "What are you doing here, Lydia?"

"Looking for you."

"Why would you do that?" His voice is low and suspicious.

I rise to my full height. Even though I barely come up to Wes's shoulder, I feel better. Stronger. I feel more like myself than I have in a long time.

"I'm coming with you."

"Lydia." He practically growls my name. "I'm not delivering you to the Montauk Project. I won't let them kill you."

"They won't. I have a plan."

He doesn't answer.

"You're going to nineteen eighty-nine, right? To investigate the election. Take me with you."

"Are you joking?" His tone is incredulous, almost angry. But I won't let that faze me.

"No. I want to go with you on your mission."

"How would that ever work?"

I pause, a little horrified at the words I'm about to say. "You haven't told them Seventeen is dead. I can take her place. I'll pose as a recruit."

"Lydia." His hand curls around my upper arm. "Why would you want to become a recruit? Why would you ever want this life?"

The wind is picking up. I hear it whip the leaves before it reaches me, sending my hair in a thousand different directions. A few red strands fall across Wes's fingers; it is oddly intimate, like I can feel where it touches his skin. "It's not about becoming a recruit, it's about getting away from this place, and . . ." I waver, but if there was ever a time to lay my cards on the table, it's now. "If we go to 1989, it will buy us time to figure out a way we can be together. A way for us to have a future."

It is not lost on me that 1989 is the year my grandfather disappeared from Bellevue Hospital. But I push that thought away. I already tried to change time once and look what happened. I don't want to risk the butterfly effect again. I just want to be with Wes.

I hear him sigh. "There is no way for that to happen. I'm

trapped in this world. And you will be too if you do this."

"We just need time." I lean in closer to him. "We can figure out how to get you away from them. The important thing is that we'll be together." His expression doesn't change, but I feel his body relax slightly.

"If we can't break you away from the Project, then I'll come back here to this time line, and you can tell them Seventeen is dead. We'll be exactly where we started. But we have to *try*."

He is quiet.

I feel myself tense, wondering what he's about to say.

"I won't do this to you. I can't." He lets go of my arm and steps back.

Why won't he at least try?

He doesn't want to be with you. The thought is a twisting coil in the pit of my stomach. "You're not doing anything to me. You're doing something *for* me. I can't be here anymore, Wes. I don't have a life here. I can't start over. I just . . . want to be with someone who knows me. Who remembers me as I really am." My voice is raw and I feel completely exposed. I shift away, staring down at the ground near our feet. "I want to be where you are. Even if we can't figure out how to get away and it's just for this one mission. I need more time with you."

"Lydia." His voice is softer. "Look at me."

I turn back to him. He searches my face, but I don't know what he's looking for.

"We can't let them win." I push my hands forward, as though the idea is a physical thing I'm holding out to him. "You know that better than anyone, especially after what you saw tonight. I refuse to let this be our fate—apart no matter what we do. I don't know how we're going to find a way out of this, but we can do something right now. We can choose each other."

He shuts his eyes as if in pain. When he opens them, there's a look I've never seen in his gaze before—something bright and wild.

He moves closer. "You might be giving up everything. Are you sure this is what you want?"

"Yes." No hesitation.

I hold my breath, waiting for him to send me away again. But then he slips his hand into mine. "I want to be where you are, too."

CHAPTER 4

Wes holds up a thin piece of metal, about half an inch in diameter. "I took this from Seventeen's body before I buried her. It's a tracking chip, and I didn't want them to find her yet."

I take it from his hand. The metal is warm to the touch and there's something slippery covering it. Blood. "This was inside of her, wasn't it?"

Wes nods, his jaw tight.

"Arm?"

"Just under the skin."

I shove it back at him, ignoring how my hand shakes. "Maybe you should put it on the inside of my arm. That will keep them from noticing the fresh wound." I hold out my left arm and squeeze my eyes shut. "Do it fast."

There is no answer, and I open my eyes again. Wes is staring at me in horror.

"You have to do it. We have no choice."

He shakes his head. "I can't. I can't cut into you."

"You did it to Seventeen."

"That was different. She was . . . and you are . . ."

"Wes, if you don't do it, they'll know I'm not one of you. Then we'll both be dead."

"You can keep it in your pocket or something." He visibly swallows.

I take the chip from him again. "I'll do it, okay? Do you have a knife?"

"Lydia . . ."

"Wes." My voice is firm. "Do you have a knife?"

He slowly reaches into one of his pockets and pulls out a Swiss army knife. I take it from him and flip open one of the blades.

I lift my arm and press the tip of the blade to my skin. It's an awkward angle, and I wince as my hand spasms, jerking the knife into my upper arm. Suddenly I feel warm, strong fingers covering my own. I look up at Wes. He guides our hands in a quick, neat movement. Before I have time to react, there is a thin incision on my arm.

I don't watch as Wes slides the chip under my skin. The cut didn't hurt much, but this does. I grit my teeth against the burning pain.

"There," Wes says softly. He reaches into his pocket and

pulls out a small, round roll of surgical tape. I hold the two sides of my skin together as he tapes it closed.

I wipe the blood off my arm. There's surprisingly little of it. "So you carry around surgical tape," I say lightly.

Wes cleans the knife off on his pant leg and then puts it back into his pocket. "I need it a lot." His voice is just as light. We are both trying to pretend the past few minutes didn't happen. "You'll need this, too." He reaches into his shirt and pulls out an ID badge. It looks like an electronic hotel key.

"It belonged to Seventeen. This will open a bunker on the northwest side. It will also get you through a few of the lower-level doors, but anything beyond that requires DNA and voice recognition. As long as you stay close to me, you'll be fine. I'll try to get us to the TM as soon as we get down there. Seventeen and I were supposed to leave this morning anyway." He looks up. The sky is still black, but the moon hangs low and heavy on the horizon. "We need to get moving. Our patrol is almost over. If we're not back soon, they'll come looking."

I take the badge from him and slip it over my head. It hangs halfway down my chest, almost the same length as Wes's watch.

"We need to hurry," he says.

"Wait." I reach up to touch his sleeve. My arm is starting to throb, a low, dull ache. "I need to know that I can pass as a recruit."

His eyes travel up and down my body and I try not to

blush under his direct gaze. "The black sweats aren't perfect, but they'll do. It helps that Seventeen had reddish hair too, though it doesn't matter much—she spent most of her time at the Center in this time period. No one should recognize her in the Facility in 2012." He frowns. "Besides, it's not like anyone pays much attention to us. Keep your eyes down, follow my lead, and you'll be fine."

"What's the Center?" I've never heard him mention anything other than the Facility in Montauk.

"A training base in New York City."

I hold my hands up. "Wait. I thought the Facility was the headquarters of the Montauk Project. Are you telling me there are more places like this?"

He must hear the dismay in my voice because he tilts his head down toward me. "Not exactly. The Center is where the recruits are trained. After the . . . reconditioning takes place, recruits are sent to New York for the other stages of training. The Facility here isn't big enough to house everyone, though this is where the paranormal experiments take place. And where the time machine is."

"The other stages of training . . . you mean tutoring, survival, and combat." I say the words like a student reciting a lesson, and Wes smiles a little. I know we're both remembering that moment in 1944 when he first told me about the Recruitment Initiative—the branch of the Montauk Project that kidnaps and brainwashes children into their puppets.

"So the kids are initially brought to the Facility here, then after they're . . ." Like Wes, I hesitate. The only word that comes to mind is *broken*, but I can't say that out loud. ". . . brainwashed, they're brought to the Center for the rest of training."

Wes nods.

"Why would Seventeen spend so much time there then? She had to have been trained years ago."

Wes starts walking again, and I move with him, struggling to navigate the dark forest. "The Center is also an outpost for recruits when we're in the city. There are sleeping quarters and weapon rooms. It's usually where we stop off before we go on any mission."

"But you must travel all over the country. Why just New York?"

"It's close to Montauk. We're less noticeable in a city, and we can travel in and out more easily." His voice changes as he says, "And it's where many of the recruits were found. There are a lot of homeless kids in New York who no one will miss."

Kids like him. "Wes . . ."

"We shouldn't talk anymore. We're almost there."

I bite my lip to keep from saying anything else.

Sometimes I feel like Wes is changing—opening up and letting me in. And other times—like now—he just shuts down. He has been living with this life for so long that I'm afraid it's like when a broken bone heals the wrong way.

The only way to fix it is to rebreak it and start over from the beginning.

But I don't know if Wes will ever be willing to relive those memories—not even to be whole again.

We walk through the woods until we reach one of the old bunkers. It looks like the one my grandfather loved to visit, the one I snuck into a few weeks ago. There's a wide, sealed door that's set in the base of a small hill. Two concrete wings frame the entrance on either side, then taper down to the ground.

"There's one other thing." Wes's voice is even lower than a whisper, and he constantly scans the woods around us. "While we're in the Facility, we have to act like strangers. You can't react to anything that happens in there. You have to hide all your emotions."

"I can do it."

His black eyes find mine. "I know you can."

Without another word, he steps forward and slides his ID badge into an almost hidden crevice near the bunker. The cement door glides open quickly and noiselessly. We slip through, and it slides shut behind us with a smooth humming sound.

We're in a small, narrow space. It's completely dark, completely silent. But even without light, Wes moves easily toward one of the walls. I listen for his footsteps and follow as best I can. In the blackness, I feel him take my hand. He guides it up to the keycard around my neck, then gently tugs. Taking his cue, I step forward and touch the wall in front of me. The cement is rough, like sandpaper on my fingers. I trace the grooves until I find a small slit in the wall. I push my card into it.

There's a low beeping sound and a light above us flashes green. A door swings open in the concrete, revealing a long staircase on the other side.

Wes goes first. I can hear his steady footsteps in front of me as we descend into the Facility. Somehow it seems even darker down here. With each step, I feel my heart pounding in my chest, my throat. All of a sudden, this doesn't seem like a very good idea. Even if we can make it through the Facility without getting caught, there's still the trip through time to look forward to—that feeling of having your body ripped apart, of every molecule splitting, separating, and getting jammed back together again. Thinking of it makes me want to turn around and run back to my safe life. *But that's not your life*, I tell myself sternly, and I keep following Wes into the shadows.

The smell hits me as we reach the last few stairs—the sharp sting of bleach and battery acid burning in my nose. As soon as Wes steps onto the floor, dim fluorescent lights flicker on, clearly reacting to a motion detector. I blink, and it takes me a minute to get used to the sudden light.

We're in a small, clean room. On each wall is a door with a black, inch-long square next to it. Wes walks over to the door furthest to his left and places his index finger down on the small pad. There's a whirring sound, like the noise a computer makes when it's booting up. I see Wes's hand twitch slightly. When he pulls back, a tiny drop of blood is beading on his finger.

An automated male voice says, *"DNA authorization complete. Voice recognition?"*

Wes leans forward. "Eleven. One. Seven. Six. Five." He is completely emotionless. There is little distinction between his voice and the one coming from the invisible speaker.

"Voice authorization complete."

The door slides open, disappearing into the wall. Wes moves through the doorway and I stay close at his back.

The door closes behind us and we're trapped inside a brightly lit small room. I turn wild eyes on Wes, but he just looks at me sharply and almost imperceptibly shakes his head. I stay frozen, waiting.

The white light around us flickers and then dies. We're in complete darkness, and I fight the urge to reach for Wes's hand. With a low hum, a red plane of light appears above us. It slowly scans the room from ceiling to floor. As soon as the light hits my head, I stiffen and close my eyes. Wes didn't say anything about them scanning our bodies. They'll know for sure that I'm not Seventeen.

This is it. I'm caught.

But Wes had to have known about these lights, that

they're not too dangerous. They're probably just scanning for the tracking chip, safely embedded in my arm. Still my body stays rigid as I feel the heat from the beam travel down my body.

Finally, the red laser disappears, and the light overhead sputters back on. A door opens on the opposite wall, and I let out a breath I wasn't aware I was holding.

We step out into a white, empty hallway. It's so bright that it makes my eyes water. It is so different from the last time I was down in this Facility; there is no siren blaring overhead and the constant red, flashing alarm has disappeared. Instead, fluorescent lights illuminate the white concrete walls, and everything is eerily silent.

There are doors on either side of us, at least ten in this corridor alone. Some are metal, while others are a cloudy glass that I can't see through. We walk down the narrow space. It bisects with two other hallways, and Wes takes the one on the right. I have no idea where we are underground, but this bunker wasn't far from the entrance I came through last time, which means we can't be too far from the TM.

Now that I'm not distracted by a screaming alarm, I notice more details about the Facility. It looks like it did in the 1940s, though the tiles on the floor and the white walls are slick and more modern. It feels almost futuristic: clean and sterile, filled with glass doors and rounded light fixtures.

I hear footsteps coming up ahead and I falter, but Wes

keeps moving forward steadily. A guard rounds the corner. He's walking toward us. *Don't scream, don't scream.* I breathe slowly and think about the ocean in summer and the beat of the waves crashing against the shore. He is right in front of us now, in what looks like an army uniform, only all black. I keep my head down, but he barely glances at Wes or at me as he walks past.

As soon as he's gone, I pull the hood of my sweatshirt more firmly over my head. The shadow of it covers my hair and most of my face. I want to smile at Wes, to touch his arm, but I can't. Instead I silently follow him through the underground corridors.

He approaches another door and puts his index finger onto the pad again. We enter another long hallway. Halfway down, a female guard with buzzed brown hair is standing in front of a wide metal door.

There's a noise like marching up ahead. Wes immediately steps back, flattening himself against the nearest wall. His eyes flicker toward me and I copy him. I stay completely still, my body pressed against the cool concrete.

The first to emerge is a guard, a little older than the girl in front of the door and carrying a large gun. Behind him, in two neat rows, come the children.

They are different ages, races, and heights, but they all shuffle forward as one body. Though they are not the same children I found in the Facility in 1944, they might as well be—half starved, vacant, with little life left in their small bodies, gray pajamas hanging off their frames. They move more like zombies than humans, completely unaware of Wes or me as they pass. It's as though we're simply part of the wall. Another piece of this place designed to hurt them.

I swallow hard as they pass us, the sound of their feet shuffling through the hallway. Wes is tense at my side. Our hands are close enough to touch. I block out everything but Wes, until I can almost feel his fingers covering mine.

Another guard marches down the hallway after them, his arms clenched around a gun. I don't let myself look after them. I can't change their fate, these children who are destined to grow up like Wes, even though I wish I could.

The hallway is clear. Wes peels himself away from the wall and approaches the guard. "Eleven," he says to her coldly. The young woman tilts her head back and then steps to the side. Wes opens the door behind her.

We walk into a lab. Several scientists are sitting around a long table, with beakers and equipment spread out in front of them. The room smells like chemicals, gasoline, and fresh paint. One of the scientists stands when he sees Wes. He is approaching old age, with almost-white hair and a bulging stomach that he can't quite hide beneath his lab coat.

"Which one are you?" His voice is low and gravelly.

"Eleven," Wes responds.

"Ah, right. Of course. Are you prepared?"

"I am ready, sir."

The scientist steps forward. He turns to look at me, and

I automatically drop my eyes to the tiled floor. "This one is going with you?"

"Seventeen is also scheduled for the mission, sir."

"They're expecting you?"

"Yes, nineteen eighty-nine has been made aware of our arrival."

"Good, good." He turns to the other scientists. They are mostly younger than him, spanning from late twenties to middle age. "Dr. Provist, please escort these two to the TM. They need to be set for August eighth, nineteen eighty-nine. Five o'clock exactly."

That's six days before my grandpa is supposed to disappear. I wonder again if it could have something to do with this rift in time. I should have mentioned it to Wes earlier, but I was too distracted, and there's no way to bring it up now.

Dr. Provist stands and leads us to a door on the opposite side of the room. We follow her out into a hallway. A guard emerges as if from nowhere and trails along behind us. I don't have to turn around to know he's also carrying a gun. We round a corner and Dr. Provist stops at a door on the left. There is a large computer screen next to it. The scientist has to press her entire palm to the black panel before the door will open. We enter the time machine room.

It looks exactly as I remember. Built-in digital screens run along the back wall, while desks with large consoles and computers sit to the left of the door. The wall to the right is a black-rimmed mirror, though I know that a narrow observation room sits behind it. I wonder who might be watching us now.

The TM is in the middle of the room. It has a tube-shaped metal frame that stretches halfway to the ceiling. The top of the machine is made of glass.

It doesn't seem to begin or end—it rises out of the floor and disappears into the ceiling. I can't suppress the shudder that runs through me as soon as I see it.

"Who's first?" Dr. Provist asks. She adjusts her glasses as she presses buttons on the computer in front of her. There's a beeping sound and the TM starts to buzz. It is so much quieter than the one I traveled through in 1944, but the vibration of it still rattles through my entire body. I can even feel it inside my head. My teeth begin to chatter.

"Me." Wes steps forward. A door suddenly appears in the smooth metal of the machine and glides open. Wes enters the hollow tube and turns to face me. Dr. Provist is too busy scrolling through codes and inputting dates to pay much attention to us. Wes's eyes lock on mine. We don't break eye contact, not until the door slides shut between us. I feel the buzzing get louder, until the machine is shaking and pulsing. The light catches above it, swirling, first white, then multiple colors, brighter and brighter. There's a moment of silence, right before everything seems to explode outward. The light is blinding, there's a numbingly loud crash. I close my eyes. When I open them again, the machine is calmer, only lightly humming now, almost like a purr.

And then it's my turn. When the door shuts, I am trapped in the darkness. I hold my breath, waiting. My heart feels like it's going to beat out of my chest. And then the floor flashes once, twice, three times. The lights are so bright that I see them even when I squeeze my eyes shut. I hear a low sound, at first quiet, but then louder and louder, until I can hear it in every inch of me. It feels at once mechanical and organic, as though this stream of noise and light and metal is coming from my own body. I hug my arms around my stomach, trying to keep the pieces of me together. But the floor falls away, and everything is suspended, and then there's a jolt and a scream. I feel myself dissolve.

When I come back into my body, I am sitting in the bottom of the machine in the pitch black. I stumble to my feet, grabbing onto the slick metal walls when the room spins. I have to be strong. This isn't over yet.

The door opens. The room beyond is dimmer than the one in 2012. Two scientists sit in front of the slighter, older computer systems. Wes is standing next to the door. His back is straight, though I see a gleam of sweat on his upper lip and at his hairline. The machine isn't something that gets easier with time.

I step out of the TM.

"Seventeen?" one of the scientists asks without looking up from his screen.

"Yes, sir." My voice is rusty, unused. I cannot remember the last time I've spoken. Not since I was outside the bunker with Wes. It feels like hours and hours ago, though it couldn't have been more than forty minutes.

"Good. Go with Eleven to the Assimilation Center. You'll depart immediately after."

My legs are like water as I walk across the room to Wes. He gives my body a quick scan, and I twist my mouth at him. It's not a smile exactly, but I hope it's enough to show him I'm okay. He returns the gesture, but he won't meet my eyes. There is something defeated in the way he holds his body, like it is difficult for him to stand up straight.

I limp toward him, knowing the pain of the TM is written all over my face. Afraid that it will give me away, I glance over at the scientists. But none of them have even raised their heads.

I was nervous they would take one look at me and know that I wasn't Seventeen, but they don't even see us. We are less than human, not even as important as the hunk of metal still humming lightly behind me.

Wes was right: it is easy to be invisible here.

CHAPTER 5

I keep my head down as we walk through the corridors. The 1989 Facility is not quite as bright or clean as it is in 2012. The walls are more of a tired beige color than a bright white. There is dust in the corners, and some of the tiles on the floor are chipped.

There are also more people down here than I thought there would be, and we pass guard after guard. I lose some of my fear when none of them even look at us. Sometimes we even pass other recruits wearing the same black spandex outfit as Wes, and I try not to stare at them. Even though they all look different, they have a similar quality in the deliberate, determined way they carry themselves. As if every action has been carefully thought out and planned.

They are too much like human robots, and so I stop

watching them, instead concentrating on Wes's back as we wind through the halls.

Despite how crowded it is, this place is lifeless. I have to think of a plan to get Wes away from here. That's why I came with him, so we'll have time to find a solution. But first we have to make it out of the Facility.

We arrive at a metal door with ASSIMILATION CENTER written on a plaque overhead. Wes pulls his own ID badge out from under his shirt and fits it into a slot near the handle. It opens immediately.

We walk into a small space with several rooms connected to it. Each door has a name above it: FINAL DEBRIEF, OUTFITTING, WEAPONRY, CULTURAL INTEGRATION.

I want to ask Wes what they all mean, but I stay silent. He leads us toward the one marked OUTFITTING, and uses his badge to open this door too.

Inside is a large room with white cupboards built into every wall. There are a few dressing tables toward the back, with wigs and makeup arranged in neat rows.

Wes walks toward the fourth door on the left. He gives me a look, then tips his head to the side. I follow his line of sight and approach the second closet.

It is filled with neat dresses, skirts, and sweaters. We are investigating an election, and that means we need to dress the part—young professionals. Uptown kids. I grab a blue dress with a wide lace collar. I start to take off my sweatshirt, then pause. Out of the corner of my eye, I glance over at Wes. He pulls his shirt off and tosses it into the open closet.

I feel my face start to heat up, but a noise near the door distracts me and I turn to see another recruit enter the room. She is about seventeen, with long dark hair and a small, compact body. Her eyes skim past me, then linger on Wes as she moves forward.

She seems different from the other recruits out in the hallway, and I watch her closely as she walks toward the other side of the room. There is a spark in her eyes, a sense of recognition as she studies Wes. And . . . something else. Something that makes me want to throw a blanket over Wes's bare chest.

I turn my back to her and peek over at Wes again. He has on dark, pressed slacks, but hasn't put a shirt on yet, and I see the muscles in his back flex as he bends over to pull on black dress shoes.

I don't like that girl looking, but I understand why she would, even if it does seem oddly out of character for a recruit. Wes straightens and I quickly unzip my hoodie. I toss it aside, then reach for the hem of my own shirt.

Can Wes see me? Will I have to be naked in front of him and this recruit? There's certainly nowhere to hide in here. How many times has this pretty dark-haired girl seen him without his clothes on? What will he think of my non-athletic body?

I grip the hem of my shirt with both hands. Wes still has

his back to me, likely trying to give me some privacy.

As quickly as I can, I pull off my clothes and yank on the new ones. By the time I'm dressed, Wes is near one of the mirrors, slicking down his newly side-parted hair. The girl recruit is taking a shirt out of the closet with her back to us. She is standing in a sports bra, completely unself-conscious. I notice that Wes is studiously ignoring her.

My eyes meet his in the mirror and he cocks his head toward one of the dressing tables. I sit down and take in the little pots of makeup and accessories.

We're aiming for uptown preppy kids. That means classy. I stare at myself in the mirror. My hair is down, streaming over my shoulders, and my green eyes seem larger than normal. The skin underneath looks bruised and a little purple.

I grab some concealer and smooth it over my cheekbones. I add blush, a light pink lipstick, and a soft green eye shadow. My hair is too messy to be tamed, so I pin it back into a low bun. Wes comes and stands over me. He nods slightly and I know I've gotten the look right.

The girl recruit turns to watch us as we walk to the door. No one speaks, but I don't miss how she leans toward Wes as he passes, like a flower opening its petals in the sun.

Back in the entryway, Wes takes a sharp turn toward the Final Debriefing room. It's a smaller space than Outfitting, with one metal desk and multiple chairs. Wes and I both sit down. There are a series of buttons in the middle of the desk. He pushes one of them, then sits back in his chair.

I covertly study him as we wait. He's wearing a blue-striped button-down that clings to his chest. A sports jacket is slung over one shoulder.

The door flies open. Wes jumps to his feet, and I mimic his actions. A man enters the room. He is middle-aged, though wearing it well: his hair is mostly brown, with streaks of gray at his temples, and the creases surrounding his eyes suggest that he smiles often.

He drops a file down onto the desk. "Eleven and Seventeen?"

"Yes, General Walker." Wes's words are quick and robotic.

"The results from a District Five city council election in New York City have changed. The original time line has a John McGregor winning by a landslide. In this new time line, he loses by a small margin. The election is won by a young candidate named Alan Sardosky." The man sounds as though he's reading off of a grocery list.

"Yes, General."

"We're sending you to New York City. Today is August eighth, nineteen eighty-nine. Up until this point, McGregor has been ahead in the polls, but something changes in the next few days. He loses momentum and stops campaigning aggressively, allowing Sardosky to inch ahead of him. By the time the election takes place, in October, he can't catch up. We need to know what happens near August eighth to affect his performance.

"As you know, time isn't always a neat package. Someone could have bumped into him in the street differently for some reason. But I want to know why and when that happens. You'll be trailing McGregor and the people he associates with in these few days. Consider this an intelligence mission. It goes without saying, you do not do anything to further alter the time line." He flips his wrist up and checks his watch. "Right now it's eighteen hundred hours. You'll be brought to the Center at nineteen hundred hours. Get the weapons and money you need before then."

He taps the file once, a muted sound. "Seventeen, you understand why you've been tasked to go with Eleven?"

Seventeen. He's talking to me. "Yes, General Walker," I say. The man finally looks up and his eyes scan my face. He stares at me for a minute, his mouth smoothing into a frown. Does he know I'm not her?

I want to sweat, to blink rapidly, to rub my palms together, but I fight against every instinct. After a minute, the general drops his eyes and I almost sigh in relief. "You were the one who discovered the error in the time line, and because of that we're allowing you to aid this mission. We haven't concluded whether or not you were the one who created this error in the first place. You will be watched by Eleven. Any misstep, and you understand the consequences."

"Yes, General." I force the words from my throat.

"Fine." He pushes the file across the desk toward us. "In this document you'll find McGregor's current address. Memorize it."

Wes flips open the folder and we both lean over. There are several papers inside, but the one on top is a blank sheet with a handwritten address on it: 32 New Street, Apartment 14D.

I repeat the words over and over in my head.

General Walker reaches over and snaps the file shut. "You're both free to go. Since you'll be in the city, you can stay at the Center. Your mission may take you elsewhere, but you need to report back here within six days. I expect a debrief by the fourteenth."

Six days to be with Wes. Six days to figure out how to get both of us free of the Montauk Project.

Wes turns to the door and I follow him. I can still feel the General's hard stare on the back of my neck long after we leave the room.

CHAPTER 6

The gun is an anchor in my pocket, weighing me to the seat. It bumps against my hip every time we hit a rough patch in the tar, and I cannot get used to its presence—not even after being on the road for almost an hour.

Wes is quiet beside me. Up front, a guard in jeans and a plain T-shirt drives the nondescript van. Before we left the Facility, we stopped at the Cultural Integration room, where a soldier gave us money and subway tokens. In the Weaponry room, they issued us both guns. I have never shot a gun—I've never even held one except for in the time-machine room in 1944—but now I have one pressed to my side. And I'm expected to use it if things go wrong.

I lean my head back against the seat and struggle to keep

my eyes open. I barely slept last night, and I've been riding a sharp wave of adrenaline and fear since I left my bedroom. Only now can I feel the heaviness of the past few hours settling down on me.

But I can't sleep yet, not while the guard keeps looking at us in his rearview mirror. I sigh and rest my hand on the seat next to Wes's leg. My fingers are spread out and reaching, wishing I could span the few feet that separate us. We haven't spoken to each other since we were in the woods at Camp Hero. We've hardly even looked at each other. I know that the distance is necessary, but it's still hard to be right next to him, unable to talk or touch.

I turn my head to look out the window. We pass a convenience store. The cars lined up by the gas pumps are all lower and longer than what I'm used to. They're sharper too, without the rounded edges that make modern cars look like oversized bugs, and the colors are duller—beige, gray, a faded blue.

I feel something move over my finger. It's so light that I think it must be a spider crawling on my skin. I jerk my head to the side, ready to swat it away. Only it's not a spider, it's Wes. He is resting his hand next to mine, so that the very tips of our pinkies touch.

I look down at our hands, then up at him. He's facing straight ahead, his expression empty. It's a look that used to scare me; he seemed so removed and closed off. But now I bite my bottom lip in an effort not to smile and I turn back to the window, hyper aware of the small place where our skin meets.

The sun is starting to set when I finally see the New York City skyline on the horizon. It is far enough away that it looks like a postcard: the buildings in lower Manhattan tower over the harbor, where clouds etched with purple wrap around the Statue of Liberty and Ellis Island.

My eyes are caught by something in the sky. Above all the other buildings, I can see the twin shapes of the World Trade Center.

I make a noise in my throat, and Wes gives me a warning look. I press my lips together to stay silent, though I don't tear my gaze away. I've seen pictures of what New York looked like with those two towers, but I've never seen them in person.

I can't help thinking about what's destined to happen here in twelve years, and I want to stop this van and grab a random person on the street and warn them. I know I can't, though. The knowledge that there's nothing I can do, no way I can help, is like a lead ball in my stomach.

We keep driving west through Queens and over the Kosciuszko Bridge. Brooklyn appears in front of us, a sprawling mass of low buildings and factories. Large smokestacks line the highway, pumping black clouds into the sky. We pass an apartment complex that is falling in on itself. It is like a skeleton: the exposed steel frame is its broken arms and legs, the hollowed-out windows its empty eye sockets.

Since New York City is only a few hours away from Montauk, Hannah and I used to take the train in for the day to go shopping or hang out around St. Marks Place. We'd buy cheap jewelry in the crowded shops or books from the street vendors. We were usually home before dark; my grandfather always worried about me spending too much time in the city alone.

But I have never seen New York like this.

We drive over the Williamsburg Bridge into Manhattan. The structure is made of beams so intricately placed they look more like lace than metal. Every surface is covered in graffiti, brightly colored names and pictures that overlap one another.

On the other side, we merge onto the highway that runs along the East River. Traffic is light, and it doesn't take us long to reach our exit. We drive under a small overpass, and I see the rounded, prone shapes of people lying beneath torn blankets and newspapers. It is almost like a village in this hidden place—ripped pieces of cloth form walls and ceilings, attached to overturned shopping carts and cardboard boxes.

A pair of street signs says 125 ST and MALCOLM X BLVD. Harlem. We pass the Apollo Theater, the red letters glowing on a muted yellow background. Our driver turns left on Fredrick Douglass Boulevard. Every other building has blackened or boarded-up windows. I can see a group of teenagers break-dancing on the corner. A crowd has formed around them, and everyone claps to the music pouring out of a boom box.

Soon the streets become cleaner, narrower. The buildings seem taller, made of gray stone and curling Baroque cornices, and there are fewer people lining the sidewalks.

Central Park starts to the left of us, and tall green trees tangle together above the stone wall bordering it. This far north the park is wilder, with no carefully manicured lawns and ice-skating rinks.

The driver pulls over near 100th Street and Central Park West. Wes and I both step out onto the sidewalk. The second the door shuts behind us, the van pulls away.

It is not yet fully dark, though the streetlamps have come on, sending a warm glow onto the pavement. I glance up at the large stone buildings above us. It seems an odd place for a government facility to be.

"Is this the Center?" I whisper to Wes. There is no reason for me to be so quiet—we're practically alone on the street. But after the hushed, secretive environment of the Facility, it feels strange to speak freely.

He smiles slightly. "No. It's over there."

I look to where he's pointing. "Over there? You mean Central Park? Are you kidding?"

"No. It's under the park. There's an entrance at One hundred and sixth Street."

"But . . . that's . . ." I sputter.

"Crazy, right?" He smiles fully this time and I see the

dimple in his cheek. It's the first time I've seen it since 1944, and I smile back at him.

"Have you heard of the Central Park Conspiracy?" he asks.

I nod. "They created a huge underground city. I remember Grant talking about it. It's supposed to be up to seven hundred acres and was used to hide all kinds of government officials. Even Hitler. They think his suicide was a cover-up, and that the government brought him here to contain him instead." I drop my voice again. "Is it true? Did it really house Hitler?"

Wes looks taken aback by the question. "No. There is a large bunker down there, but it was built for the Montauk Project."

"I guess the conspiracy wires got crossed."

Wes opens his mouth, but he doesn't say anything.

"What is it?"

"Grant . . . told you about this?"

I tilt my head at him. "Yeah. So?"

"Nothing, I . . ." He looks away from me.

"Grant was my—Lydia's—boyfriend in this time line," I say carefully. "I assumed you knew about that."

"I did."

"Well—" But I'm interrupted as an older woman walking a very small dog passes us. The dog yips at my ankles and I step back to avoid getting bitten.

"Sorry," the woman apologizes. "He's usually so

friendly. Aren't you, Pookie? Aren't you?" She leans down and makes a kissing noise.

"No problem," I mumble. But the moment between Wes and me has passed, and for the first time I realize how exposed we are out here. This area might not be very crowded, but we should probably get off the street.

I take Wes's arm and pull him back, away from the woman and her dog. "Are we sleeping in the Center tonight?"

He nods, clearly distracted by something.

"Is there anything I need to know? Like any laser body scans you might have forgotten to mention?"

He straightens at my accusing tone. "I'm sorry it scared you. They were scanning for your tracking chip, not for our identity."

"This Center . . . what's it like? Will anyone recognize that I'm not Seventeen?"

"No. There are two wings—the training area and then the quarters for recruits and soldiers. Recruits can come and go as they please from that section."

"I don't understand." I don't bother hiding my frustration. "If you can come and go as you please, then why don't you all just leave?"

"And go where?" Wes's voice is detached. "I told you this before—most of us never had a family, and those who did have forgotten them long ago. There's no point in guarding something that wouldn't escape even if it could."

"But *you* do have something to escape for." My voice is

rising, and I see a young couple turn to look at us.

"Lydia, they will find me. I never have more than a few days out of the Facility, and then only for missions. You heard the general—we have to report back in six days. And it better be worthwhile information, or we're as good as dead. If we don't show up, then they come looking. And when they find us they kill us or make us wish we were dead." Wes is maddeningly calm.

"There has to be a way," I say harshly. "We will find a way."

His mouth tightens the smallest bit, but he doesn't answer. We stand there staring at each other.

He is the first one to break the silence. "Come on, we need shelter for the night. Tomorrow we have to start investigating McGregor."

I thought he brought me here so we could figure out how to break him free, not so he could complete General Walker's mission. But I don't push it, at least not yet. Instead, I say, "Fine," and follow him across the street.

On the other side, I step closer to him and our arms bump together by accident. It's the first time we've really touched in hours, and the contact makes him stop walking abruptly. I turn to face him. A heavy lock of black hair falls across his forehead, impervious to the gel he put in earlier. I slowly lean up to brush it away.

He peers down at me, his brows drawn. Then he grabs my arm and pulls me along the sidewalk.

"I thought the entrance was the other way." I have to shout the words. He's walking so quickly that wind whips across my face and pulls at the pins holding back my hair.

"There's something I need to show you."

"Wes, wait." I tug on my arm until he's forced to stop or let go of me. "You have to talk to me."

His eyes are wide, and his skin seems stretched too tightly over the bones of his face. He seems to be vibrating with energy. It's so different from how he was a few minutes ago that I tense, afraid something is wrong.

"I used to live near here." His voice sounds the same, and I relax slightly. "Do you remember what I told you by the beach?"

I think back to our conversation that night in 1944: the open door of his jeep, my knees almost touching his stomach as he leaned toward me. "Yeah," I say, a little breathlessly. He said he was living in an abandoned subway station uptown with some other orphans.

"I want to take you there."

"Won't they miss us at the Center?"

He shakes his head quickly. "The general will track us using our chips, but even he understands that these missions can take you to unexpected places. We can't always get back to the Center to sleep. As long as we don't disturb the time line, it doesn't matter. But we don't have to . . ." His voice falters, and that strange gleam leaves his eyes. "We can go to the Center now, if you want. It'll be dark soon."

I take in the stiff way he's holding himself. "This is important to you, isn't it? You want to show me your home."

He looks down at the uneven cobblestones at our feet. "It's not really a home, not like you know it. But it's the place I remember the best. We stayed there for years. I missed it, after they took me. And . . . I want you to see where I'm from."

I put my hand over his and hold on tight. "Take me there."

The station is dirty and brown—tiles are falling off the walls and the paint is chipped. Wes and I slip our subway tokens into a metal slot and go through the turnstile. There are people all around us; a train must have just arrived. I feel the ground rumble and vibrate as it departs.

It smells like sweat and urine, and I try not to breathe as we walk all the way to the end of the platform. Up ahead is a wall and some stairs that disappear down onto the tracks. Wes looks over his shoulder, but there are only a few people standing near the turnstiles and none of them are paying us any attention. He quickly hops down the steps. I take his hand and follow him into the underground subway system.

It is even hotter down here, like black pavement in summer that spent all day in the sun. Sweat gathers along the back of my neck. I want to fan myself, but I also don't want to let go of Wes's hand—the only thing guiding me through the dark.

We travel along the edge of the tracks, on a narrow stretch of dirt close to the wall of the tunnel. There are tall black columns every few feet, and we skirt around them as we walk.

"As long as we stick to the right side we're fine," Wes whispers to me. "The third rail is the only one that's electrified."

"What happens if a train comes?"

"We die."

His words startle a laugh out of me, and the sound echoes through the enclosed passageways. "I seriously hope you're kidding."

I can hear the smile in his voice as he says, "Don't worry. If a train comes, we'll have enough room to squeeze against the wall and wait it out."

He stops talking as we reach a fork in our path, where the rails twist in different directions. "Careful. There are some live wires here."

A dim yellow bulb overhead sheds a small amount of light onto the ground. It's not much, but I can see Wes's feet as he steps around the interlocking metal rails. I slowly trace his path, using his hand to steady myself.

After a few more minutes of walking, we come upon a door set in the wall not far from the tracks. It is rusted and partially falling off its hinges. Wes pulls it open enough for me to squeeze through, and I crawl into a long, skinny room covered in graffiti and grime. The air smells sour and heavy. There's a small, faint light set high in the ceiling and another door at the far end.

Wes enters the space behind me, and he quickly strides to the opposite door. He grabs the rusted handle but looks back at me before pushing it open.

I stop in the middle of the hallway, watching him. "Are you okay?"

"I haven't been here in a long time."

"How long?"

His knuckles are white on the metal door handle. "Not since I came back for my watch. That was over four years ago."

"There's no one living here anymore?"

"No, they all abandoned it years ago."

"Were there a lot of you?" I edge closer to him.

"A few of us. We looked out for each other. I don't know what happened to them." He sounds a little too casual, like he's trying very hard not to show that he cares.

I am finally close enough to reach out and touch his hand.

His fingers spasm, probably with how hard he's gripping the handle. I meet his eyes and hold them as I push gently on both our hands. The door swings open slowly.

I wait until Wes breaks our gaze, his dark eyes scanning the small room. He is in a daze as he enters—it is one of the few times I have seen him act without those careful movements.

The room is almost empty, with piles of dirty blankets in one corner and an overturned chair lying in the middle of the floor. The walls are made of large, old bricks, some of them falling out and breaking into dust.

Wes kicks at the blankets and something inside squeaks. I jump back as a large rat scurries out and disappears into a hole in the wall. Wes keeps his back to me, and I wonder if he's ashamed that this is where he came from.

I want to tell him he doesn't need to be, but I don't know how to say the words.

He crouches down and rifles through the pile. "Here," he whispers, pulling something out and holding it out to me. It's an old and stained comic book. I take it from him carefully. "Batman, February nineteen eighty-three," I read. "Wes, you've been holding out on me. I didn't know you were a comic-book nerd."

He smiles. "I liked them. Never had any money though. I stole that one." He says it defensively. "I must have read it a hundred times."

I trace the picture of Batman fighting a clone of himself on the cover. *Struggle as hard as you want, Batman—you can never defeat yourself*, it says.

"It was one of the only other things I had that was mine." I look up. Wes has moved in that silent way of his, and he's standing next to me now, staring down at the comic in my hands. "Aside from my watch."

I touch the metal pendant that's hanging against my

chest. "Do you want it back?" I ask softly.

He raises his eyebrows. "No. I wanted you to have it. That's why I gave it to you."

"Good. I'm getting attached."

He smiles again and takes the comic book back from me. "I missed this. I missed being here. Weird, right?"

I glance around the small space. It's cooler here, away from the heat-generating trains, but it still feels like a coffin—dark, windowless, and buried far beneath the ground. But if it was the only home you ever knew . . .

I move into him until my shoulder meets his chest. "I think it's great. I'm glad you brought me here."

His face is serious as he says, "Me too."

I smile, and he clears his throat. "We should get going, though."

"Okay." I have no idea how late it is, but we need to sleep if we're going to face whatever tomorrow brings.

Wes hides the comic book again, and we leave. I go first, pretending not to notice how he lingers in the doorway.

Soon we are in the subway tunnel, walking back toward the station. We reach the complicated point where the subway tracks cross in a mess of rails. I watch Wes again, copying where he steps. I've almost reached him when my foot catches on an exposed rock and I begin to fall. I raise my hands instinctually. I'm about to smash into one of the tracks, when I feel myself come up against something hard. Wes's arms close around my body and he pulls me to the side of the tunnel, pressing my back to the rough wall.

I wonder why he doesn't let go, until I feel the walls start to shake. There's a low grating noise that gets louder and louder, accompanied every now and then by a long screech. Suddenly a white light is facing us, coming closer. A warm wind picks up and then the train is on top of us, speeding past, faster than I could have imagined, loud and bright and so close that I could touch it if I reached out.

Wes tightens his hold on me. I feel one of his hands on the back of my head, pulling me into his chest. Both of my arms are around his waist, my hands resting on his cotton blazer. He shifts and his fingers weave through my hair, tugging on it gently until my head is tilted all the way back. His face is distorted in the flashing light of the train, but I can see his eyes—so black they look like liquid. He leans in. I keep my eyes open, locked on his, closer and closer. He hesitates for a second, only an inch or two away. I can feel his fingers hard against the back of my head, and I bite my bottom lip. His gaze drops down at the movement, and then his mouth is on mine.

I grip his jacket tightly in my hands and press closer to him. He deepens the kiss, and I feel his tongue touch mine. His hand frames the side of my face, fingers lightly tracing my cheek, and I can't help but sigh against his lips.

We kiss as the train rushes by: the screaming noise, the interior lights of the cars, the passengers standing against the doors holding newspapers and wishing they were already home. We kiss as sparks kick up when the train turns the corner, yellow spots of light that die out before they can even reach the ground.

It feels like both a second and a hundred years. We finally come up for air, gasping a little, and I realize that the subway tunnel is dark and quiet again. Wes must realize it too, because he pulls away. I stare up at him, not sure if my ears are ringing from the passing train, or from the feeling of being pressed against him.

I was afraid I had forgotten what it felt like to be kissed by Wes—the soft pressure of his lips, the low sound he makes in his throat. But as soon as his mouth touched mine, it all came flooding back.

He steps backward until he's close to the tracks. My breathing sounds loud now in the empty tunnel, and I press one hand to my chest.

"We need to keep going. You must be tired."

"Wes—"

He shakes his head as if to clear it. "We have to get some sleep. There's a lot to do tomorrow."

I suddenly feel cold, even though it's like a sauna down here. I take a shaky breath, and Wes turns away from me.

Why is he acting like this? Why does it feel like he's pulling away, right when we found each other again?

I follow him out of the subway tunnel.

CHAPTER 7

As soon as we reach 106th Street, Wes stops. We are near the entrance to Central Park, and three sets of stairs lead into the trees beyond. "Stranger's Gate," I say, reading the mossy-covered word that's carved into the adjacent stone wall.

"Fitting, I think," Wes responds softly. He holds his body separately, stiffly, in a way that I don't quite understand. He brought me on this mission. He trusted me enough to show me his old home. Why would kissing me change that?

I assumed that when we came to 1989 together, it would mean we would be *together*. But maybe I was making assumptions I shouldn't have.

"The access point is over there." Wes gestures toward a small stone building near the gate.

"Let's go then." I try to keep any emotion out of my voice.

"Wait—" He grabs my arm and I freeze at his touch. "The Center is a big place. It's watched and monitored like the Facility, but there are a few spots where we can speak freely, if we're careful. I'll let you know."

"Okay."

He pauses, and I wait to see if he'll say anything else. But he just releases my arm and turns to face the park.

We walk up the first set of steps, then veer off the path and over to the small stone building. If I didn't know any better, I would think it was an abandoned toolshed or something. I glance around us, but the sidewalk is mostly empty and the streetlight overhead has been vandalized, the bulb hanging in tattered pieces of glass. It's probably deliberate, a way to keep people from noticing the recruits entering and exiting.

We circle the building until we're in the shadows, not visible to anyone from the park or the street. There is a heavy black metal door on the side. It appears to have no handle and no way to open it. Wes takes out his ID badge and slides it into a slot between the stones. The door pops open. We quickly enter the small space, sealing the entrance behind us again.

It is pitch-black inside, and when I try to walk forward I trip over something. A rake, or a shovel. Maybe this is a toolshed after all. Or maybe that's just a good cover in case someone manages to find their way inside. I hear the sound of plastic brushing against stone, and I realize Wes is running his fingers over the opposite wall looking for another slot.

He finds it: I hear the swipe of his card and then a low grinding noise. Light floods the small room as a door opens in the stone, and I see a dimly lit stairwell that descends into the ground below the park.

With a strong sense of déjà vu, I follow Wes down the steps. From somewhere nearby, I hear the sound of water dripping, and the walls around us are dotted with green and brown mold. At the bottom of the stairs is another heavy-looking door. Instead of a black pad for DNA authorization, it has a simple keypad next to it. Wes inputs a ten-digit code. The door slides open to reveal a small room.

I expect to be scanned again, but as soon as we enter the space, the door shuts behind us and a computerized screen appears on the wall. Wes pushes a button marked FLOOR 9, and we drop so quickly my stomach flips over. The Center is deep, deep below the park, probably even lower than the subway systems. No wonder no one ever finds this place.

We reach our floor with a jolt, and the door in front of us glides open again. The dim hallway we step out into is lit with sputtering fluorescent lights, and the musky, mothball smell makes me wrinkle my nose. It feels like a sewer system down here; the ceiling is a curved, wide arch, and there are exposed pipes running along the walls.

We turn left out of the elevator. The hallway abruptly ends at a wide metal door. Wes inputs another ten-digit code and it opens slowly.

In front of us is a long, gray hallway. It is sleek, made of chrome and glass—so different from the entryways we just passed through. The ceiling is still curved, but that's the only similarity: this wing of the Center looks like a fancy office building transported hundreds of feet below the ground.

There are several people in the hallway. I stare at my feet as we walk forward, praying that no one realizes I'm not Seventeen. When we pass a black-uniformed guard, my whole body tenses and I press my palms into the scratchy material of my dress. But he barely notices us.

We pass several recruits, and like Wes and me, they are in clothing from 1989. Some are dressed like punks, complete with piercings and Mohawks. Some are dressed in bright pink tops and white sneakers. They look like normal teenagers, though their blank eyes give them away.

A few doors dot the walls on either side of us, but Wes ignores them. He moves through this place fluidly, assertively, and I realize he must have spent a lot of time here. As if to prove me right, he suddenly stops at a completely nondescript door and uses his ID card to open it. We enter another hallway. This one also has several doors attached to it, and Wes uses his keycard again to open one on the right. Inside is an empty room with two sets of metal bunk beds tucked onto either side of the walls.

The door shuts behind us. I feel Wes's breath near my ear. "This room isn't bugged. You can speak, though try not to move your mouth much. There are cameras."

"Okay," I breathe.

There's another door on the back wall, and Wes walks across the room to open it—to my relief, it's a private bathroom.

"You can change in here if you want." I have to walk halfway across the room in order to hear what he's saying. "Clothes are there. Put your dress aside, you'll need it for tomorrow." He cuts his eyes to the right and I see shelves lining the walls, covered with neatly stacked black clothing.

Keeping my movements brisk, I pick some clothes from the shelf and go into the bathroom to change and wash my face. By the time I come out, Wes is lying on the lower bunk of the bed closest to the door. His eyes are closed, his breathing steady, and I can't tell if he's asleep or not.

I crawl into the lower bunk right next to his, and lie so that our heads are close together. We can't see each other, but if I reached out, I would touch his hair.

It has been almost a day since I last slept, but I lie awake, staring at the metal bottom of the bunk above me. The room is bright—the lights never seem to go off in these places—and after a while it makes my vision blur.

"Are you awake?" I hear Wes whisper.

"Yes." The word sounds slurred as I answer him without moving my mouth.

"Tell me about your life now. What happened after you got back to two thousand twelve?"

"You don't know? You always seem to know everything."

I hear a rustling noise, like he's turning over. "I watched you sometimes, when I was in Montauk and could get away. You seemed . . . happy enough."

"I've been pretending. With everyone."

"Tell me, Lydia. I want to know."

So I tell him about my parents, about Hannah, about missing journalism, about Grant. Wes breathes more sharply, but he doesn't say anything. It is hardest to explain about my grandfather, but I manage to get the words out without crying.

"I'm worried that it's my fault," I whisper. "I was the one who lost Dean, and now Grandpa is in Bellevue because of me."

"You didn't choose to go back to nineteen forty-four," he replies. "It was an accident."

"Yeah, but once I was there, I chose to try and change the future, even though you tried to stop me. And now . . . I don't want to screw up anything else."

"Is that why you're not asking me to help you save your grandfather?" He sounds curious.

"I guess so." I twist onto my side, facing the gray wall.

"I don't want to tempt fate anymore. I learned my lesson."

We are both quiet for a minute.

"Lydia . . ."

"What?"

"Do you have feelings for him?" His words are soft and I can't tell what he's thinking.

I tilt my head up. "Who? Grant?"

He doesn't answer.

"No. Of course I don't." It is a struggle to keep my voice low.

"You kissed him."

"I had to. I didn't want to disrupt time again."

"Maybe he's—" Wes falls silent.

"What?"

"Maybe he's better for you. Than someone like me." His words are muffled, as if he's speaking into the pillow.

"I don't want him. I want . . ." *You.* But after he pushed me away in the subway, I'm afraid to say the word.

"What about you?" I ask instead. "I saw the way that girl watched you."

"What girl?"

"The dark-haired one in the Outfitting room."

"You mean Twenty-two?"

"I guess so." I cross my arms over my chest.

As though he can see the movement, Wes says, "She's just another recruit, Lydia. I've never even spoken with her. You're the first person I've . . . since . . ."

Oh, Wes.

"I know," I whisper.

There's a pause. "We should sleep."

I close my eyes and listen to him breathe. "Good night, Wes."

"Good night, Lydia."

I wake up to Wes lightly touching my shoulder. "Time to go," he says.

I feel as though I haven't slept at all, and I stretch my arms over my head as I sit up slowly. "Okay," I mumble, then freeze. I've forgotten where I am for a moment.

At my expression, Wes slightly tips his head back. I look over his shoulder. There is another recruit in the room, a girl asleep on the top bunk of the opposite wall. Her short blond hair tangles around her face. In her sleep, she looks peaceful, like a normal girl.

I stand up and pull my dress off the end of the bunk. The gun is no longer in my pocket, and I wonder if Wes took it out at some point, knowing that its presence made me uncomfortable.

When we're both dressed, Wes leads me to another Outfitting room. This time I don't avert my eyes every time we pass a soldier or a recruit.

We're the only people in the room. I quickly fix my makeup while Wes tries to tame his hair, though I know that in a few hours the thick black strands will just be hanging in his face again. By the time we're done, we look like two yuppie kids from 1989.

Breakfast is served in a large mess hall. Wes and I sit across from each other at a low table. We don't talk. No one does, despite how many recruits are in the room.

We leave the Center the same way we came in, through the sewer room, up the elevator, back up the dirty staircase. Soon we are standing on the sidewalk of Central Park West.

When the sunlight hits me, I shut my eyes tight. "You okay?" Wes asks when he sees my face.

I squint at him. "It's too bright."

A shadow falls across my cheek. Wes is holding his hand up high, using it to shield me from the sun. I give him a half smile, and he smiles back, just as tentatively.

"I guess we should go to McGregor's apartment first," I say. "We need to at least keep up the pretense of your mission for the time being."

Wes lowers his hand. He seems distracted as we start walking toward the subway station. "We have to find out where McGregor is for the day, what he's doing, and who he's seeing," Wes says. "It's the only way to find out how the rift happened."

"You mean aside from me somehow altering the past in nineteen forty-four."

He gives me a look. "Obviously."

I grin at him. Now that we're out of the Center, I feel like I can breathe again. And despite the fact that I'm not sure what's going on with Wes, I'm in a surprisingly good mood.

"And all we have to go on is his address." I look up at the sky. There is only a small stretch of blue visible, the rest taken up by buildings and trees. "Thirty-two New Street. Apartment . . . Fourteen B?"

"Fourteen D."

"What would I ever do without you?" I say, only half joking.

Wes flashes his dimple at me. "What has gotten into you?"

"I'm happy." I shrug. "You're alive. I'm alive. And we have six whole days together."

"Five now." He sounds serious, but his eyes crinkle at the corners and I know he's amused.

"Five days! That's a lot of time to figure out how to get you away . . ." But I don't finish the sentence as I see his face darken. He starts walking a little more quickly, and I hurry to catch up with him.

"Wes, wait. I'm sorry." I touch his arm and he stops. "I don't know what's going on. I thought you wanted to be free of them. Isn't that why I'm here? Isn't that why you brought me?"

He goes still for a moment, his head turned away. Finally he looks at me, and his expression softens. "I'm sorry. I know I'm not . . . this is just hard for me."

"I get it. I do." I drop my hand. "Let's concentrate on

McGregor right now, okay? We can deal with the rest later."

"Yeah, okay." His lips tip up, though the smile never reaches his eyes. "Let's check out that address."

We step out of the subway and into the heart of the Financial District.

"I didn't think anyone even lived down here," I say as I stare at the men and women walking quickly down the sidewalk, briefcases by their sides. "I thought it was just office buildings."

A balding man knocks into me, but I catch myself before I stumble. "What time is it, eight? Everyone must be heading for work."

Wes frowns. "Let's hope McGregor is too." We push through the crowd until we find a space between two buildings. Thirty-two New is right across the street, and I look up at the fourteenth floor. I can't see anything but row after row of mirrored windows.

"We need a plan," Wes says.

"Let's go up there, knock on his door. If he's there, we say we're Jehovah Witnesses and leave. Wait till he's gone again. If he's not there, we break in and see what we can find."

"Pretty simple."

"You got a better idea?"

Wes shakes his head. "Remember, we're trying to have as little contact as possible with him. We don't want to alter the time line further."

"What happens if we do, by accident or something?"

"Time can always be changed again. As long as I can prove it wasn't deliberate, then they won't punish me. But I'd have to tell General Walker in my debrief, and they would send another recruit back to this exact moment to stop us."

I glance back and forth, but no recruit materializes out of the sea of briefcases. "Looks like we're good."

There is no lobby or doorman in McGregor's building, just a locked front door. I start to pull a pin from my hair so I can open it, but Wes stops me. "Hang on," he says. "That will take too long." He pulls out his Swiss Army knife.

I watch, fascinated, as he covertly opens one end, like he's taking the cap off a pen. Underneath are a bunch of pins sticking straight up. Wes pushes them into the lock. Some collapse while the rest mold to the keyhole. I hear a clicking noise, and then Wes turns the knife like it's a key. The door opens.

"I want one of those," I say as we enter the building.

"You could have gotten one in Weaponry."

"Don't tell me that now, it's just mean."

He laughs softly and I smile. I love making Wes laugh; he does it so rarely.

We take the elevator up to the fourteenth floor. The hallway outside McGregor's apartment has dingy carpet and dull yellow lighting. It's not where I would have expected a politician to live.

When we reach 14D, Wes knocks twice. There's no answer. I put my ear to the wood, but I can't hear anything moving in there. "I don't think he's home," I whisper.

"Let's find out."

Wes pushes the pins into the lock. It clicks a few times, and I slowly turn the door handle.

It opens into a studio apartment. There's no way McGregor is home; there's no place to hide in here.

"I'll take the desk," I say quietly.

Wes walks over to a file cabinet near McGregor's bed and opens it with a creak.

I glance around the small, masculine space. It's as though he just moved in: only one chair sits near the counter in the tiny kitchenette area. His bed is covered with a faded red blanket. Nothing hangs on the walls except for a blue sports banner.

I walk over to look at the pennant more closely. It says EAGLES in white letters. There is something familiar about it that I can't quite place.

I leave it and move to examine his desk. A black leather notebook sits on one side. I open it and flip through the pages. It's a datebook.

"Wes, look at this."

He comes over to join me near the desk. "It's all of his appointments for the week." I angle it toward him.

"Where is he now?"

I find Wednesday, August 9. "Right now he's . . ." I trail off.

Wes leans over me. "Visiting Bellevue Hospital." He steps back and rubs at the corner of his jaw. "Lydia, do you think—?"

But I don't answer, because I have finally realized why that pennant looks so familiar. It matches one that was hanging on the wall in Dean's room in 1944. The Eagles. My East Hampton High School football team.

"John McGregor is from Montauk." I pronounce each word slowly. "Wes, do you know how old he was?"

He shakes his head. "I was looking for a birth certificate, but it's not here."

"It doesn't matter." I sit down on McGregor's bed, holding his datebook close to my chest. "They stopped making those pennants ages ago. He had to have known my grandfather. Maybe even Dean." I look up, my eyes wild. "Wes, you know what this means. McGregor's loss could be connected to my grandfather."

"Or we could have affected his fate somehow when we were in nineteen forty-four. If he was in Montauk then, it's possible." He comes to kneel in front of me. "You don't know your grandfather is involved."

I squeeze the datebook tight. "He must be. John McGregor is visiting someone in Bellevue right now. I'm betting it's him."

Wes suddenly goes tense. His eyes dart over to the door. "Lydia, we have to leave." He jumps to his feet and tugs me across the room. "Someone's coming."

I hear the sound of keys jingling in the hallway, and I throw the datebook back onto the neat wooden desk. It lands with a thud that I'm sure is noticeable, but I don't have time to care. Wes has opened the tiny window in the kitchen, and he waves me through.

I duck down and out onto the fire escape. Wes is right behind me. We pull the window shut as the front door swings wide-open.

We both press against the side of the building, breathing hard. "Too close," I whisper, and Wes nods. He starts to climb down the fire escape, but I stop him.

"Lydia . . ." Wes murmurs as I crawl under the dingy window ledge.

"Hang on a second." I slowly lift my head until I can see into the apartment. McGregor has his back to me, and is roughly yanking off his tie. He turns slightly, and I duck, but not before I see his profile and the weary look on his lined face.

He's a small man, with almost dainty shoulders and dirty-blond hair. But he's broadly handsome in a way that reminds me of a Kennedy. No wonder he went into politics.

"We should go," Wes breathes, but I shake my head at him. I wait a beat, then peer into the window again. McGregor is lying on the bed with his feet planted on the floor. He has one hand pressed to his eyes, and the other is clenched in the red blanket beneath him. He looks completely crushed; I wouldn't be surprised if he were crying.

I drop down and crawl back over to Wes. He gives me an exasperated look, and then swings his body onto the fire escape stairs. I follow him, but I can't get the image of McGregor out of my mind. Whomever he was visiting at Bellevue left him devastated.

If it was my grandfather, then that means he's somehow involved in this rift in time. And that means his connection to the Montauk Project runs deeper than I ever imagined.

CHAPTER 8

You know what the next step is, don't you?"

I sigh. "We have to go to Bellevue and talk to my grandfather." I must sound as defeated as I feel, because Wes turns to face me. I ignore him and stare out at the Statue of Liberty. The water around it is choppy and the waves peak on crests of white foam.

"I'm not sure I'm ready."

Battery Park is practically deserted at nine in the morning on a Wednesday, though I spot the occasional tourist wearing a green foam Statue of Liberty crown. We are by the water, right where the ferryboats pull into the harbor. I find something soothing about the way the water splashes against the dock beneath us. Maybe it just reminds me of Montauk, of home.

Wes leans on the railing next to me, deceptively casual. "I think you are ready. I—" He stops.

"What is it?"

His mouth twists. "I think it's part of why you wanted to come to this time period with me. So that you could find him."

I straighten. "No! It's not, I swear. I came for you."

"I believe you, Lydia. But I also *know* you, and you're not one to run away from the things that scare you. Maybe, deep down, you were hoping something like this would happen so it would force you to face your grandfather's disappearance."

I turn away from him and run my fingers violently through my hair. Some of the pins holding it in place scatter, making tiny *pings* as they hit the pavement.

Since when did Wes become a shrink?

But as much as I hate to admit it, I have been running away from the consequences of what happened in 1944, and it's not like me. I do want to at least *see* my grandfather. I need to face the reality of this new time line I helped create.

And besides, I miss him.

"You're right." I look back at Wes. "Of course you are. I want to see him again. But I also want to help you get out, Wes. That *is* why I came."

He faces away from me, staring out into the park. There's a group of break-dancers setting up not far from us. A teenager drops his boom box on the concrete while another one flips over onto his hand, his legs at right angles in the air above his body. Wes seems absorbed in the scene, and I wonder if he even heard me. Finally he says, "We can't abandon this mission. We have to keep looking into McGregor so I have information to bring to General Walker when this is all over."

I don't say what I'm thinking—that if we can get him out of the Project, then he'll never have to be debriefed about what happened here. But I understand why he's hesitant, why he feels the need to cover all of his bases in case we don't succeed.

"I'll help you however I can," I say to him. "If that means we need to complete this mission, then I'm here for you. But—"

Before I can finish, he looks over at me. "Then it looks like we *have* to go talk to your grandfather. You can see him again, and we can find out the connection between him and McGregor."

I nod, but then bury my face in my hands. "You're right. I just wish I didn't have to dump the Montauk Project on my grandfather's doorstep again. I wanted to keep him out of it this time."

"I think he's already in it." Wes sounds grim. "How soon does he disappear?"

I lower my hands, gripping the metal railing until it stings my palms. "On August fourteenth. In five days."

"The same amount of time Walker gave us to complete our mission."

"And now my grandfather is probably connected to

an election that is somehow vital to the Montauk Project. That's a lot of coincidences."

"I don't believe in coincidence," Wes says. "Not anymore."

We take the subway to 28th Street. Bellevue is almost all the way to the East River and we have to walk a few blocks before we reach it. The streets are teeming with people, and I concentrate on the back of Wes's striped shirt as we navigate the busy sidewalks.

"Yo!" The shout pierces through the noise of the traffic and I lift my head. But it's crowded out here, and I can't see who yelled.

"Yo, man!"

It sounds even closer this time. Across the street an African-American boy is waving at . . . us?

"Hey! I see you, man!" He hops into the street, mindless of the oncoming traffic. A car blasts its horn and I see the driver throw up his hands. The boy is getting closer, and I stop walking. He looks about our age, and he's wearing red shorts and a white T-shirt that's covered in bright splashes of paint. Wes stops too, staring out into the street.

"Wait up!"

There's a dark-haired girl standing on the sidewalk watching us. Suddenly she lifts her head and her whole body tenses.

"Yo, We—" But the boy is cut off by the girl's shrill voice.

"Tag!" she shouts. He pauses in the middle of the street and turns back to look at her. "Cops! Let's go!"

The boy wavers, glancing at us, then back at the girl. I see his chest rise and fall as he sighs, and then he runs over to her and grabs her hand. They disappear into the crowd just as a cop car pulls up. Two officers in dark blue uniforms spill out. I crane my head to see what happens, but Wes puts his hand on my back, urging me forward.

"What was that?" I ask him as we start walking again.

He shrugs, though I notice that he's staring back at where the boy disappeared.

"Did you know him? Was he yelling at us?"

"No. Come on. We're almost there."

"Wes." I stop walking and look up into his face. "Are you sure you're okay?"

"I'm fine, Lydia."

"It's just that . . . your eye is twitching."

He jerks his hand up and covers his eye. I watch as his face convulses, as though all his muscles just stop working at once.

"Are you okay?"

"I said I'm fine!" He snaps the words as he turns away from me.

I automatically take a step backward—Wes has never spoken to me like that, and I don't know what to say. Finally he faces me again, slowly lowering his hand. His eye looks a little red, but otherwise he seems normal.

"Sorry," he says quietly.

"I was just worried about you." I sound defensive.

"I know. I'm sorry," he repeats. "I really am fine." He reaches down and grabs my hand. I let him hold it, and I don't say anything when I notice he's shaking.

Bellevue Hospital sprawls along the east side of the city. Over the years it has been added to and adapted and now it is a series of tall buildings made of glass, concrete, and red brick. A black wrought-iron fence still sections off the original buildings. There is something creepy about the dark metal juxtaposed against the modern glass structure.

Wes and I find the entrance and approach a wide front desk.

"We're looking for the psychiatric ward," I tell the young female receptionist. "My . . . uncle is a patient there."

She doesn't look up from her desk. Her hair is a teased, puffy blond cloud, and her nails are long and red. "Emergency room or committed."

"Committed."

The word makes her finally lift her head. "How long?"

"About four weeks now."

"Psychosis or drugs and alcohol related?"

I swallow. "Psychosis."

"You want Unit Nineteen North." Her voice is a little softer. She quickly gives us directions.

We walk through a few hallways until we reach an elevator. The car we get on is filled with people, and we have to squish together just to fit.

As soon as we get off on the psychiatric ward, the atmosphere changes. Instead of a busy hallway, with doctors and staff and patients teeming the halls, this place is quieter, more deserted. In the distance I hear someone shouting.

We approach a heavy metal door with a red button on it. I push the buzzer and hear someone fumble with a lock on the other side. The door opens a little, and a male nurse in pale blue scrubs sticks his head out. "Yes?" he asks.

"We came to see Peter Bentley," I reply. "He's a patient here?"

The man frowns. He is young, though the fluorescent light overhead bounces off the dark, shiny skin of his bald head. "Is he expecting you?"

I shake my head. "But he's my uncle," I add.

"It's visiting hours, isn't it?" Wes asks.

The man scratches his bushy eyebrow, then looks over his shoulder. I can only see a little of the room behind him. It has white walls and shiny beige floors. "Wait a second," he says. The door shuts, and Wes and I are alone in the hallway.

After a minute the door opens again, and the nurse gestures us forward. "We don't usually let visitors into this area," he says. "But Bentley is a special case. We can't move him right now. Keep your hands to yourself and don't talk to any of the other patients."

I exchange a glance with Wes before we step into the psychiatric ward. The nurse locks the door behind us with a key. We're standing in a long, wide hallway. Directly across from us is an open entertainment room. I can hear a cartoon on the TV in the background, with loud, exaggerated sound effects. To our right is the main nurses' office, with glass windows that look out onto the hallway.

There are a few patients roaming around, some accompanied by nurses, some alone. A woman with taped-up glasses and wild hair sees us hovering near the doorway. "I hate this place," she says, her words slurring. "It doesn't work. It doesn't work." Her voice is getting louder and louder. A nurse comes forward and takes her arm, steering her back down the hallway.

"Welcome to the loony bin." The male nurse laughs loudly, a booming sound. Wes and I are both silent.

"This way," he says, still chuckling.

The hallway has a few pictures, cheerful landscapes in gold frames. Though the walls are white, the doorways are painted a sunny yellow. I remember reading that color can affect mood, and that yellow is supposed to make people feel happy and productive. I wonder if it actually works.

We pass a door with the word SECLUSION written above a narrow window. Inside, a man rocks back and forth on a mattress on the ground, staring at nothing. I slow down as I watch him, wondering who he is, and if my grandfather has ever ended up here in this room. Wes must feel me pause, because he turns around and follows my gaze. His face softens, and he steps back until he's close enough to whisper in my ear. "Are you sure you want to do this?"

I straighten my shoulders and nod. His hand finds the small of my back, and together we walk down the hallway toward my grandfather's room.

The nurse pauses at a door and turns to face us.

"He might be tired," he says. "He had another visitor this morning."

I exchange a glance with Wes. "Who was it?"

"Some distant cousin. Maybe you know him since you're Bentley's niece. A John McGregor?"

I press my lips together. I'm not surprised to hear that my suspicions were correct—McGregor and my grandfather are connected. But a distant cousin? It might explain why McGregor was so affected by this visit, though is it enough to make him lose the election?

"Yeah, I know him," I say slowly. "A politician, right?"

The nurse shrugs. "I don't know. But he was pretty upset when he left. That can happen sometimes, when visitors aren't prepared for the state their friends and family are in." He looks both of us over. "Just . . . be ready."

"Okay," Wes says. I don't answer, in no way prepared for whatever I'm about to find on the other side of this door.

The nurse knocks. There's no response, but he opens the door anyway.

"Mr. Bentley?" he calls out into the room. "You have another visitor. She says she's your niece."

There's a groaning sound, and then a muted thump, like a body turning over in bed. "Have no niece," a scratchy voice responds.

I gasp. It sounds rusty and low, but that is definitely my grandfather's voice.

"Of course you don't," the nurse says soothingly. "But why don't you talk to the pretty girl anyway?"

There's no answer. The nurse steps back from the door. "Go on in," he says. "He's not dangerous to anyone, and he's having a good day. I'll be just outside the door in case you need me."

I cannot move, so Wes nods for us and takes my hand. He tugs me gently, and I step forward. The room is bare—there are only two beds pushed against opposite walls, and two freestanding wooden closets. A big, white lump occupies one of the beds. The other bed is empty and neatly made.

I slowly walk forward. The rubber soles of my shoes squeak against the linoleum floor. As I get closer, the white lump turns into the outline of arms and legs, a rounded middle, and finally a head with black and gray hair that sticks up out of the blanket.

The head turns and looks up at me. I squeeze my hands into fists, and my breath comes shallow and tight. This man looks like a stranger, with his longish curly hair and snarling grin.

And then something in his face changes, calms, and I want to throw myself against him. This is the man who helped raise me. One of the people I love most in the world. My grandfather.

CHAPTER 9

*G*randpa."

Wes makes a warning noise in the back of his throat, but I hardly notice.

The man in the bed narrows his eyes and his face changes again, looking feral and suspicious. "What did you say, girl?" he spits out.

"Uncle," I amend quickly. "It's good to see you again, Uncle."

His eyes sweep up and down my body, landing on my face. "I don't know who you think you are, but I have no niece. Have no brothers or sisters. You're no relative of mine." He cocks his head, staring at me intently. "Though the eyes are right. You've got Bentley green eyes."

"I am a Bentley. Lydia Bentley."

"Lydia." He makes a humming noise. "I knew a Lydia once, when I was a small boy. She had red hair, too."

My mouth falls open and I turn to Wes. He's frowning. "You must be confused." His voice is hard. "Lydia is your niece. That's where you recognize the name from."

Grandpa sits up in his bed and waves his hand in the air. "I know, I know what you all think of me. I'm 'confused.' I can't hold on to reality. But it's not true. They're the ones who can't see what's right in front of them." His eyes glaze over, and he starts to smooth the blankets down around him. "So what are you doing here, oh niece of mine?"

It takes a moment for me to speak. He's younger than I remember, but has the same long face, with high cheekbones and a full mouth. But his hair is not completely white like I'm used to, and he's not wearing his wire-rimmed glasses. He must be around fifty now; his face is mostly unlined, though there are deep grooves around his mouth and eyes.

I met my grandfather in 1944, when he was just a small boy. It was strange to see him as a child, but in a way it was easier than this; he felt like a completely different person then. Now he is enough like the man I remember that I cannot separate the two people in my head. But this version is too young and too angry. It's like looking through old, wavy glass where the image on the other side is only slightly distorted.

"I, um . . ." I clear my throat. "We don't want to tire you

out. We heard you already had a visitor today."

"I'm not tired."

He doesn't say anything else, so I try to prod him in the direction of McGregor. "Was your visitor someone close to you? Another family member?"

"*Another* family member? I thought we established you're not my family."

"But this visitor was family?"

"McGregor?" His voice becomes lighter. "Son of my great uncle, don't know what that makes him. Second or third cousin, I guess. Known him all my life."

"Does he visit you often?"

"First time I saw him in years. No one comes here." His eyes cloud. "Not even my son anymore."

I glance at Wes.

"Did you know McGregor was a politician?" Wes asks.

"'Course I know that! Running for city council." Grandpa turns his head to the side, as though dismissing us.

I take a small step closer to the bed and say the first thing I think of. "Why don't you tell me a little bit about your childhood? About how long you've known McGregor."

But it's like he doesn't hear the second part of my suggestion. He looks over at me again, and I flinch at the manic gleam in his eyes. It reminds me of those few times I saw him get like this when we were at Camp Hero. Did he always have this person lurking somewhere inside of him?

"My father disappeared when I was young." His voice is

slow, a little dreamy. "I knew they did it. I knew it. I went looking. I spent my whole life looking."

"Looking for what?" I can't help but ask.

"For *them*. She said he was bad, but she was wrong. He was the victim. They were the villains. She knew he was part of it."

"Who said he was bad?"

"Lydia."

I whip my head around to look at Wes. He frowns, and I know we're both remembering that day in the woods behind my great-grandparents' house, when Peter overheard me talking about Dean and the Recruitment Initiative. In a fit of anger and confusion, I did say that Dean was the bad guy. Is that the moment that I changed the course of history?

"Later I knew. I found the journal. I read what he wrote, and I knew that she knew something. But she was gone too. I searched for him, for them both."

"But you didn't find them," I say, my voice small.

He smirks. "Who says I didn't find them?"

"What does that mean?" I lean forward, McGregor and the election forgotten.

Grandpa's smirk turns into a wide smile. He really does look crazy, with his wild eyes and long, messy hair. Like the Mad Hatter from *Alice in Wonderland*.

"What are you saying?" I move even closer to him and the wide neck of my dress slips to the side, falling down over one shoulder and exposing my upper arm. I start to yank it back up, but my grandpa reaches out and grabs my arm.

His face is pale. "You have it. You have the mark."

"What are you talking about?" I try to pull away, but his fingers are claws that dig into my skin.

"The mark." He wrenches his gaze away from my arm. His eyes focus like lasers on Wes. "Do you have it too?"

Wes steps forward, ready to pull me away.

But Grandpa lets go of me on his own, throwing my hand to the side like my skin is radioactive. "Who are you?" His voice is higher. He sounds horrified. "You've come for me, just like you came for him. I know too much, don't I? I know too much."

I back away from Grandpa, stopping when my body hits Wes. His hands come up and close around my shoulders.

Grandpa is starting to thrash in the bed, twisting from side to side. "You're one of them!" he screams. "Don't take me! I'm not ready! I'm not ready!"

I press my hands to my open mouth. What did I do? Why is he acting like this? The door bursts open and two nurses rush into the room along with two members of hospital security.

"Hold him down," one of the nurses says.

The two security guards grab his arms and torso. He struggles against them, still screaming. "You have it! The mark! You're one of them!"

Wes and I back away, moving as one unit. His hands tighten on my shoulders.

They are strapping Grandpa to the bed using cloth ties. A doctor in a white coat enters the room carrying a large syringe. She presses the needle into the pale skin of my grandfather's neck as the guards hold him down.

"This will help calm you, Peter," she says in an even tone. I almost don't hear her over his shouting.

I feel someone touch my arm, and I jerk to the side. But it's just the male nurse from before. "You better go," he says.

I nod and follow him to the door. My grandfather's screams have become whimpers. He is no longer shouting, but his breathing is heavy and labored.

I turn back to look at him right before I leave the room. He is staring at me. "You have it." His words are garbled, as though some invisible force is strangling him. "The mark of the traveler."

The nurse leads us to the main exit. The door to the nurses' station is open and the hallway is empty—all of the other nurses on duty must be in with my grandfather.

"Sorry about that," the bald nurse says as he steps into the office. He starts to rummage through a drawer, most likely looking for the key to let us out of the ward.

I blink rapidly, trying not to cry. "What's wrong with him?"

"He has a delusional disorder."

"A what?"

"It's a rare psychological condition where a patient becomes obsessed with some wacko idea and lets it take control of his life. It's odd though—he has no record of past psychosis. Our patients usually have a long history of being in and out of hospitals." He shrugs. "But sometimes it can come on later in life. It's just a shame that he can't stay here anymore."

"He can't?"

"We're not a long-term care facility. We try to rehab our patients and stabilize them enough to enter society, but I don't think that's an option for your uncle. . . ."

I don't either, based on what I just saw. "Where will you send him?"

"Rockland State Hospital, probably."

Wes glances back in the direction of Grandpa's room. "Is there any way for us to see his files?"

The nurse shakes his head. "Only his doctors have access to those. Not even family."

There's a loud banging noise, and I hear screaming coming from a nearby room. "Excuse me," the nurse says. "I have to check on that. Wait here, okay? I'll unlock the door for you in a minute." As soon as I nod, he takes off down the hallway at a sprint.

I turn to see Wes watching me carefully. "Are you okay?" he asks.

"Not really."

"I'm sorry." He reaches out and traces the curve of my

cheek with his finger. I close my eyes at his touch, but he drops his hand quickly.

"The last time I didn't believe in him, it turned out he was right. I thought he might have some answers, but he's so different from the grandfather I knew." I shake my head, wishing I could erase the past few minutes from my brain. I thought seeing my grandfather would make me feel better, but . . ."He's like a stranger. What do you think happened in there?"

Wes's expression is dark, his mouth turned down at the corners. "I don't know. He freaked out after seeing your scar." He gently pushes up my sleeve, exposing the small, round mark on my upper arm.

"You have a matching one." I put my finger on his arm, touching the stiff material of his shirt. "I saw it back in nineteen forty-four when we were in that cell in the Facility."

He looks down at his arm, surprised. "I do have a scar there. Just like yours. I never put it together."

"Is it where your chip is implanted?"

"No, that's here." He pulls up his sleeve to expose a thin silver line on the inside of his arm.

"He called our matching scars the mark of the traveler. You've never heard of it before?"

"No."

"How old were you when you got yours?"

He frowns. "I don't remember getting it, but I first

noticed it after I was already taken in by the Project."

"Then why would I have it too?"

"I don't know." Wes's voice drops. "But McGregor, your grandfather, these marks . . . Something is going on. We need more information."

"They won't let us see his file, and we're not going to get anything else out of Grandpa. At least not now."

"We need to know what he knows."

I look down the empty hallway. Grandpa is a dead end. If only we could see his file.

My gaze falls on the open door of the nurses' station.

"I have an idea."

Wes raises an eyebrow. "What are you thinking, Lydia?"

"Just cover me."

I creep into the open door of the office. There are windows along the front wall that look out into the hallway, so I duck down and crawl along the floor until I reach the file cabinet. I find the A-E section and try to open it. It's locked. Of course.

Wes is standing in the doorway with his arms crossed over his chest. He's alternatively watching me and scanning the area around the office. I spin around on my heels.

"Toss me your knife."

He pulls it out of his pocket and throws it at me.

I yank the cap off the end and insert the pins into the lock. It gives way with a small popping sound. I smile up at him. "I love this thing."

He smiles back. "I'll get you one."

"You better." I rifle through the names until I find *Bentley, Peter*. I pull out the thick folder. Behind the file is a plastic bag with his name on it, so I pull that out, too. I slide the folder into the neck of my dress and throw the bag at Wes. He unties his sports jacket from around his waist and hides the plastic bag in it. I slam the drawer shut and just manage to dash out of the office before the nurse comes back around the corner.

"Sorry about the wait," he says cheerfully. "Ready to get out of here?"

"Definitely," I answer.

We sit down on a sidewalk bench, facing each other. I pull the folder out of my dress and put it between us. Wes drops the small bag next to it, and I peer through the clear plastic. It holds a belt, shoestrings, and a copy of *The Metamorphosis*.

We don't speak as we each take a section of papers from Grandpa's file.

I find a handwritten note and start to scan it: *Peter is more lucid today, though he still shows signs of his delusion, even after putting him on Haldol. Up his dosage?*

"Do you know what Haldol is?" I ask Wes.

"I think it's an anti-psychotic," he answers absently as he rifles through my grandfather's admission papers.

I turn back to the notes. *He is obsessed with a conspiracy theory called the Montauk Project, and worries that "they" are coming after him. It is built on his continuous claim that he recently saw and spoke with his late father, though he has been missing and presumed dead for the past forty years.*

"Wes, look at this." I show him the passage I just read. "There's no way he could have talked with Dean, right?"

"I don't know." Wes stares down at the paper. "Dr. Faust claimed that Dean was sent to the nineteen twenties, but it was an old machine and Dean wasn't very young. He could have traveled anywhere in time."

"If he survived it, which is unlikely." I remember the files I found back in 1944, of all the soldiers they tried to send through time. I forget sometimes, that the Project isn't all bad; in the beginning they were trying to send those soldiers on missions that would help them prevent World War II by killing Hitler. But even then, human life wasn't as important as the mission, and the TM had turned those men into vegetables, if it didn't kill them immediately. That was before they realized children have a better chance of making it out alive.

"Some of those soldiers did survive the traveling, they just got lost somewhere in time," Wes says. "Not all adults die from the TM."

"I guess it's possible that the TM screwed up and sent Dean to the eighties instead of to the nineteen twenties."

Wes frowns. "But how would your grandfather have seen or talked with him, if he was brain-dead and under surveillance by the Project?"

"I don't know. How could my being in the past affect McGregor's outcome? What is the mark of the time traveler?" I drop the paper back down and press one hand to my forehead. "I'm so sick of all these questions."

We're sitting on a bench on a narrow side street. Every now and then, people walk by and yellow cabs pass, but it's like we're in our own world, hidden from the crowded, noisy city.

"You like answers." I can hear the smile in Wes's voice.

I drop my hand and look up. "Of course I like answers. Who doesn't?"

"You're kind of obsessive about it, though."

I bristle at his words. "Well, I want to be a journalist. It comes with the job."

He tilts his head, his dark eyes finding mine. "I didn't mean it as an insult. It's fascinating, to watch you try to puzzle all of this out."

I feel myself start to blush, and I look down at my lap. "Life was a lot easier when I was interviewing cheerleaders and writing exposés on cafeteria food. This is a little out of my depth."

"Lydia." His voice is low. "I'm so sorry that you got caught up in all this. If I hadn't—"

"Saved my life?" I cut in. "Wes, you haven't done anything but help me. I don't regret what happened. I . . ." I hesitate.

He breaks the moment by sitting back quickly and

picking up the clear plastic bag. "What's in here?"

I sigh, but take the bag from his hands and open it slowly. "I think it's the stuff Grandpa had on him when he was brought in to Bellevue." I sift through the shoestrings and the belt, knowing that they took them from my grandfather so he wouldn't try to hurt himself, and pull out the only other item—Franz Kafka's novel *The Metamorphosis*.

"I read this in tenth grade."

Wes takes it from me and examines the cover. "What's it about?"

"This guy wakes up and realizes he's been turned into a giant insect. And even though he feels the same on the inside, everyone is disgusted and starts to treat him differently."

"What happens to him?" He hands it back to me.

"He kills himself, to spare his family from having to deal with him anymore." My fingers clench around the paperback, until I'm almost bending the spine in half. "I guess it makes sense why my grandfather had it, huh? He didn't wake up as a cockroach, but the world can't relate to what he became."

"Lydia . . ."

I shake my head. "I'm okay." I flip through the book to distract myself. My grandfather has written in the margins here and there, and I realize it's a pattern: SO4N2H11C9O-C9H11N2O4S. The same one he wrote over and over in the journal I found on Lydia 2's desk.

Why does he keep repeating the same sequence over and over? What does it mean to him?

I find something else toward the back, tucked in between the pages. It's a folded newspaper clipping. I pull it out and set the book aside, aware that Wes is watching me closely.

I open the crumpled paper. It is a clip about a rally that took place near Riverside Park on the Upper West Side. I scan the words, but they mean nothing to me.

In the bottom corner there's a small, grainy photo. I hold it up higher, angling it toward the light. It's a picture of the rally, with groups of people marching past a large building. There are wide steps leading up to an ornate front door. It looks like a hotel, but I can't really be sure. A man stands near the entrance, wearing a fancy uniform and a small hat. I squint at his face and turn to Wes in horror. The man in the photo looks exactly like Dean Bentley.

CHAPTER 10

Why would there be a picture of Dean in a newspaper clipping from February 10, 1989? I shove the paper at Wes as my mind races through the possibilities. Is it even him? Maybe it isn't.

"That's Dean." Wes's voice sounds resigned, and I wonder if he can ever be shocked by the Project anymore.

"How is this possible? Why would a soldier from World War II end up working at some hotel in nineteen eighty-nine?"

"I don't know."

I gather all of the papers and stuff them back into the folder. "We have to find this place. We have to talk to him. Maybe it's just someone who looks a lot like Dean."

"Maybe," he says, though he doesn't sound like he

believes it. "Seeing this might be what sent your grandfather to Bellevue."

I stand up. "Or what made him come to New York in the first place. He left Montauk around the end of February. He was hunting his father."

Wes stands too and faces me. "But the question is, did he find him?"

"If he did, then wouldn't Dean have recognized him?"

"Not if he was brain-dead after his trip through the TM."

"But why would he be working as a doorman if the TM destroyed his mind? It doesn't make sense."

"And it also doesn't explain what 'the mark of the traveler' means."

"No, it doesn't." I look down the street, at the quiet brownstones and the green, canopy-like trees. "And I don't know if it's connected to McGregor. I don't want to pull you away from your mission, but . . ."

"But this is something you have to do," he finishes. "I understand, Lydia. It's your family."

"I can do it alone, if you need to focus on McGregor," I offer, but he shakes his head.

"I think all of this is connected to McGregor. It's not like we're chasing down some false lead."

"True." I tap the folder against my leg. "I wonder if McGregor knows what 'the mark of the traveler' means. Maybe my grandfather mentioned it to him too."

"I think it's time we talk to McGregor. It seems like

his losing the election had to do with your grandfather in some way, which had to do with the reason he ended up in Bellevue—"

"Which had to do with us being in nineteen forty-four," I finish. "But that's not information you can bring to your debrief with General Walker. Not without giving us away."

He tilts his head. I was right—his gel has officially given up and a piece of black hair falls down into his eyes. He brushes it away with a quick movement. "No, but there could still be another reason he loses his election. We won't know until we talk to him."

"We should talk to McGregor first, then. If he's not connected to all of this"—I sweep my hand out, indicating Grandpa's files—"then we might as well close that door before we go see Dean."

Wes gives me a look. "Are you sure you're not just avoiding Dean?"

My heartbeat picks up at the thought of seeing Dean again. I may have had a hand in his disappearance, but if it really is him in the photo, then at least I didn't get him killed. But still, to see him again and remember that moment when he disappeared into the TM, and the pain of imagining him ripped apart in time. To think of how it must have affected Mary and her parents and Lucas, forever left wondering what happened to him.

"I can't decide if I want it to be Dean, or if I don't." My voice is quiet.

"It'll be okay, either way."

It's not a promise he can make—I know that—but it doesn't stop me from smiling at him as we stand up and head toward the subway.

We can't bring Grandpa's files with us to visit McGregor. They're too bulky and too obvious—the name *Peter Bentley* is printed all over them in large red letters. If McGregor sees them, he's bound to get suspicious. It's not an aspect of the butterfly that I'm willing to chance, and Wes suggests we drop them off at his old home in the subway.

"Are you sure you want to go back there again?" I ask him as we walk down the sidewalk. "I know it was . . ." I search for the right word. "Hard for you."

He's quiet for a moment. "It's fine. I like the idea of using it like it still belongs to me."

I touch his wrist lightly. "Let's go then."

We take the subway back to 103rd Street. The station is different during the day, buzzing with life and noise and energy. It is harder to sneak onto the tracks; we have to wait for a train to come and go, until the platform is mostly empty.

We move quickly through the underground tunnels. No trains pass, but I hear one far away, rumbling the walls next to me and causing small pieces of dirt to fall from the ceiling down onto my hair.

When we reach Wes's hideout, he pries open the outside door for me and I duck into the long hallway. I move forward, not waiting for Wes to join me. But as soon as I clear the other doorway, I skid to a stop.

The room isn't empty. Two people are sitting on the floor with their backs to the wall. They stand up as soon as they see me.

Wes comes up behind me more slowly. He's moving with that deliberate prowl, probably sensing long before me that we weren't alone in here.

"Yo." One of the intruders steps forward.

As he says it I recognize the boy who called to us in the street. His black hair is closely cropped, and he has a neat line shaved along one side of his head, twisting up around his right ear and ending at his temple.

The girl is still with him. She's standing near the wall, watching us with narrowed eyes. Wes moves out of the doorway and stands next to me.

"I knew it was you." The boy grins widely with bright white, crooked teeth. His features are just a little too blunt to be handsome, though the corners of his mouth naturally tilt up, as if at any moment he's about to break into a grin. "Where have you been, man?" He steps closer to us, his arm outstretched.

"I think you're mistaken." Wes's voice is so cold that even I shrink away from him a little bit.

"What are you talking about? It's me. Tag." The boy laughs a little. "Don't tell me you don't remember."

Wes is silent.

"Come on, man. *Tag.* Remember Izzy and Little Pop and Jake? You're here, aren't you?" He gestures around the darkly lit room.

What is he talking about? Could Wes know this person?

The girl eyes me. She stands with one leg thrust in front of the other, her arms crossed. She sees me looking and her mouth twists, like she just tasted something sour.

Tag is shaking his head slowly back and forth. "Wes, man. I know you remember. Where the hell have you been?"

My mouth falls open. He knows Wes's *real* name. I thought I was the only person in the world who knew Wes's identity before he was taken in by the Project.

Wes was kidnapped in 1984 when he was only eleven years old. If he had stayed in this time period, he would be . . . sixteen in 1989. The age Tag appears to be now. This kid is someone from Wes's old crew, someone who recognizes him even after all these years.

I look up into Wes's face. He's still frowning, but there's a spark in his eyes I've never seen before. He recognizes this person, probably did from the minute Tag started yelling at us on the street. But all of his training is forcing him to deny it. To push away anyone who might try to get close to him.

My hands curl into fists. I refuse to let him keep closing himself off. Not from me, or from Tag, who cares enough about Wes to track him down here.

"Wes," I say softly. He tears his gaze away from Tag and

looks down at me. "It's okay."

Tag and the girl are watching us, but I tune them out and rise on my tiptoes so I can whisper into Wes's ear. "No one has to know if you remember him. The Project will never find out. You can have a piece of your old life back."

I rest my hand on his chest for leverage as I lean closer to him. I feel his heartbeat under my palm. "It's okay." I repeat the words, breathing them into his ear. "You're not alone anymore. I'll keep you safe."

Long dark eyelashes sweep across his cheeks as he squeezes his eyes shut. He sighs and I feel the tension leave his body in a heavy rush. His hand comes up and fists in my hair, holding me close to his chest for a minute. Then he lets go and steps back.

"Tag." His voice is rough. "I remember you."

"Of course you remember me, man. Who could forget Tag?" He steps closer and holds his hand out.

Wes hesitates for a second before he reaches out. The boys slap palms, bump fists twice, then pull their hands back with their fingers spread wide.

A secret handshake that neither forgot.

Laughing, Tag slaps Wes hard on the back. He's about six inches shorter than him, and he has to reach up to clasp his shoulder. "It's good to see you. Where you been?"

"It's a long story," Wes responds. He sounds different—he has the slightest New York accent that wasn't there before.

"I haven't been down here in years." Tag does a small

spin, taking in the pile of blankets, the single overturned chair. "Not since you left. We're mostly all downtown now. No wonder we haven't run into you, if you've been crashing up here." He gestures toward me. "This your girl? She's fly."

Wes doesn't answer. I look down at the dirty floor. There's a silence that should be awkward, but Tag laughs through it. "Yeah, man, you haven't changed. Still all quiet and shit. Don't let anyone know your business."

I turn to Wes in surprise. I thought his stoicism was something the Montauk Project instilled in him, but maybe Wes always kept his emotions to himself.

"This place is whack." Tag wrinkles his nose at the blankets in the corner. "You can't stay here. Come crash with us. I'm pretty set up right now. Squatting over near Avenue D. Rigged up electricity and everything, man. You got to see it." He looks over his shoulder, suddenly remembering that he didn't come alone. "Nik, get over here."

The girl slides forward. She's not exactly pretty, but her sharp features and her large brown eyes give her an innocent, appealing quality.

"This is my old pal, Wes. We used to hang with the same posse. Wes and me known each other since we were practically babies."

"That so?" Her voice is high and a little squeaky. Kind of like a frightened bird. She keeps her arms crossed and her mouth pursed as she stares at Wes and me. All attitude.

It's a strange contrast to her cartoonish voice and cherubic features.

"Wes, this is Nikki. She's been hanging with me for a while." Tag hooks his arm around Nikki's neck. They're about the same height and both rail thin.

"This is Lydia." I feel Wes's hand touch my shoulder. It's so different from the way Tag curls Nikki into his body that I glance away, swallowing hard. When I lift my eyes, I see Nikki watching me carefully. She gives me a knowing look before she turns back to Tag.

"Nice to meet you, Lydia." Tag grins. There's something infectious about it, and I find myself smiling back at him.

"You too."

"So what'll it be?" Tag asks Wes. "You gonna stay in this shit hole, or you gonna come back to our crib?"

Wes and I exchange a glance. We're supposed to be visiting McGregor. But we have five days before our time is up. And Wes has been alone for so long . . .

Wes's mouth is drawn, and I know that he's about to turn Tag down to focus on our mission.

"We'll come," he says.

I jerk in surprise.

Tag grins even wider. "Wicked. Let's go now. LJ's on dinner tonight, and he always manages to find the good stuff." He takes Nikki's hand and leads her to the exit.

Wes turns to follow them but stops when I grab his arm. "You agreed to stay with them, just like that?"

"Do you not want to?"

"No, I mean, I do, but . . ." I push my hands up through my bangs. "It's just not like you. To agree so quickly. I thought I'd have to talk you into it."

He smirks at me, a very un-Wes-like look. "Well, now you don't have to."

He disappears through the door. I stare at his back, wondering what's gotten into him. That strange moment with his eyes twitching, that manic look when he was dragging me toward the subway, and now agreeing to put off the mission? Wes is not acting like himself.

But if it means he's willing to open himself up to his old memories, is that necessarily a bad thing? Maybe he doesn't need to rebreak the bone like I thought. Maybe he's healing all on his own.

We walk up through the East Village and turn onto a side street off of Avenue C. I edge closer to Wes as we pass homeless kids in roving gangs, old men passed out in doorways, and drug dealers camped out on every corner. They shout at us as we pass. "Coke, smoke? Coke, smoke?" they shout when we walk by.

The buildings on both sides are tall and imposing, throwing deep shadows across the sidewalk. Most of the windows are smashed out or have thick metal grates over them. It already feels like night here, though the sun hasn't even set yet. I see a drag queen in a huge pink wig tottering down the concrete in stiletto heels. She disappears into a sunken doorway.

Tag and Nikki stop in front of a large brick building. It looks like an abandoned tenement, with several stories and boarded-up windows and doors. Graffiti, bright and garish, sweeps across the light-colored brick.

"This is it." Tag points at a basement window, where two wooden boards have been pried off and tossed to the side.

Nikki goes first, crawling through the small space. She disappears into the blackness beyond.

Wes walks forward and braces one hand on the frame as he slides in the window. The fluid way he folds his body is too graceful, too perfect. It's easy to see that he has been trained in some way: no one is born able to move like that.

I turn to see Tag watching the spot where Wes disappeared with narrowed eyes. "I guess he's learned some new moves."

Before I can say anything, Wes calls out, "Come on, Lydia."

I slide through the window, and Tag follows. The dark room around us is filled with junk—empty bins and crates, old furniture covered in dusty tarps. The only light comes from the cracks between the boards that cover all the windows.

"This way." Tag leads us through a doorway and to a tall staircase. We climb up three flights. I can't see much, just the impression of small hallways and battered doors. The entire building smells stale, like moth-eaten sweaters or an old basement.

Finally, Tag stops on a landing and flings open one of the doors. A warm light pours into the hall.

Tag and Nikki disappear into the doorway, and Wes and I follow. The room around us is filled with *stuff*. Candles and bottles and blankets and furniture.

"It's like the cave of wonders from Aladdin," I say under my breath. "Without all the gold."

Wes smiles slightly. "More like the cave of forty thieves."

Tag and Nikki move around the room, turning on even more of the lamps. The room is practically glowing. You'd think they'd want to be a little more subtle, considering they're here illegally, but I guess not.

The apartment is bright and cluttered, with boards pulled away from the windows to let in more light, and lamps scattered all over the floor. They are connected by a series of wires that disappear out one of the windows. I tilt my head down and see that it's attached to one of the power lines outside. This must be how they're getting their electricity; they're sucking it off of the main city grid.

"What do you think, man?" Tag spreads his arms out and spins around a little. Though clearly not trained like Wes, he still moves with an easy sort of grace. It makes me wonder if he's a dancer. Or maybe just a really good fighter. "Beats our old haunts, huh?"

Wes looks around the room, and I know his dark eyes are taking in everything—the two connecting doorways with sheets draped over them like curtains, the lawn chairs next to a cheap plastic table. The walls look like they've been attacked with color, as though someone painted them in rage: lines are splattered and slashed across the once-white background, stretching from the floor all the way to the high ceilings.

"There's a shower in our room," Tag says, pointing toward one of the connecting doors. "If you guys want to take one. LJ—he's Nikki's little brother—figured out how to hook up the plumbing, though we have no gas so the water's always cold."

"Can I take one now?" I ask, aware of the last two days of grime covering my skin.

"Sure. I think Nikki has some girly soap around. Right, Nik?" Tag looks at her.

The dark-haired girl scowls, but doesn't disagree.

"Will you set her up?"

Nikki walks into the bedroom and I follow her. The painted walls are even darker here, with large gashes of color.

"Did you do this?" I ask.

She shakes her head. "Tag."

"Really?" I'm surprised; he doesn't seem capable of such dark emotions. But then, he did spend his life on the streets. Maybe his cheerfulness is as much a mask as Wes's detachment.

Nikki shoves a towel at me, and I walk into the cramped bathroom.

The water is freezing. By the time I get out, my teeth are chattering and goose bumps have taken up permanent residence on my arms and legs.

I pass Wes in the bedroom, and give him my towel. "Will you tape my arm again?" I ask.

He nods, and carefully reapplies surgical tape to the wound. It is angry and red and stings when he touches it. "I think it's getting infected," he says softly.

"I'll be fine. They have antibiotics in the eighties, right?"

He smiles at my sarcastic tone, then moves into the bathroom. I stare after him as he shuts the bathroom door. He seems more natural here than he was in the Center, or even in 1944. It's a good thing that we decided to stay, though I still don't know what made him agree to it.

Nikki and Tag are at the large table in the main room.

"Thanks for letting me shower," I say. "I almost feel human again."

"Don't mention it." Tag gets up and pulls out a chair for me. "LJ should be here with dinner soon."

I sit down. "So you knew Wes when you were kids?"

"Yeah, known him forever. I ran away from a shitty situation as soon as I could." At my sympathetic expression, he shrugs. "No one missed me, and it was better than ending up in the system. Wes was already living on the streets. He was practically born here. Don't know how he ended up without parents. He doesn't either." Tag's tone is a little too casual.

"We found each other and decided to team up. Kids

barely old enough to feed ourselves, fighting for territory and begging for scraps. We fell in with some older kids for survival, but we mostly looked out for each other. Then one day, poof!" Tag wiggles his fingers in the air like a magician on a stage. "He disappeared."

I lean forward. "Didn't you worry about what happened to him?"

"Sure. But I figured he got picked up by the cops, or got tossed in a home. It happens. People disappear all the time out here." His gaze cuts to Nikki and he falls silent.

"What was Wes like back then?"

Tag smiles. "You ask a lot of questions, huh? Miss Twenty Questions. That's what we'll call you."

"No," Nikki interjects. "Princess. It's a better name for her, don't you think?"

I narrow my eyes at her, but before I can say anything, like *screw you*, the front door of the apartment swings open.

A younger boy is standing there. He looks like he's about thirteen or fourteen, and he drops a heavy bag down on the floor where it lands with a thud. "I got soup."

Tag gets up and looks inside the backpack. "Rad. Only slightly bruised. You go Dumpster diving?"

"Yes." He sees me sitting at the table and he goes still and watchful. There is a wounded air around him that makes me want to put my hand out, like I'm approaching a scared animal.

Nikki stands up from the table. "LJ, this is Lydia. She's with him." She points toward Tag's room, where Wes leans

143

against the door frame, his hair wet and sticking up around his head. I notice he's wearing a clean black T-shirt; Tag must have given it to him.

"That's Wes," Tag says. He's sitting on the floor, heating up the cans of soup on a small hot plate. "He's an old friend of mine."

"Nice to meet you." LJ keeps his head down. He has darkly tanned skin and large brown eyes, and I feel like I recognize him from somewhere. He does look like Nikki, though he doesn't have the same pointy features that she does. But I can see the similarities in their round faces, their doe-like eyes.

"Soup's on," Tag calls out. "Literally."

Wes straightens from the doorway and walks over to the table. He sits next to me, and I smell soap and pine trees.

Tag puts a bowl in front of each of us. Wes and I eat slowly, but the rest of them shovel it into their mouths. I wonder if it's the first meal they've had today.

"It's your turn on dishes," Nikki tells LJ when all the food is gone.

He straightens, making his lean body look even skinnier. "I did them yesterday."

"Nice try." Nikki ruffles his brown hair as she gets up from the table.

The sky outside is dark; the sun has finally gone down, and the room is filled with a soft light. I start to yawn, and the movement spreads through my entire body.

Wes sees it. "You're tired."

"A little."

"Why don't you sleep?" He turns to Tag. "She can have the couch, right?"

"Yeah. LJ crashes in the other room, and Nikki's in with me."

LJ catches the tail end of the conversation as he comes back into the room carrying an armful of dishes. "There's another bed in my room," he tells Wes. "You can have it if you want." His voice squeaks on the words and his face gets red again.

Wes shakes his head. "I'll take the floor."

Tag scoffs. "Why would you do that? There's a free bed."

Wes looks over at me. "I'm fine on the floor."

I stand up and walk to the couch. It smells a little like body odor and mold, but I curl up on it anyway. "Wes," I mumble. "I'm fine out here. Just go sleep in LJ's room." I close my eyes.

I don't hear his response. I'm almost instantly asleep.

CHAPTER 11

In the middle of the night, I wake to the sound of hushed voices. My eyes crack open. Wes and Tag are sitting at the table. There's a bottle of something between them and they're passing it back and forth and taking small, wincing sips.

Almost all of the lamps have been switched off except for a small one that rests near their feet. It gives off just enough light to see their bodies, but their faces are blurs of shadow.

"I haven't had this stuff in years," Wes says as he takes a sip of the dark liquid. "God, it still burns, huh?"

Tag laughs sharply, then stops abruptly and looks over at me. I squeeze my eyes shut, but Wes just shakes his head. "Don't worry about her. Lydia's a heavy sleeper."

It is strange to hear Wes talk about me with someone

else, and I stay perfectly still, trying to catch every word.

"How'd you two hook up?" Tag asks. "And don't give me some shit about not being together. You never stop looking at her, not even for a second." He laughs softly. "I remember how it used to be. Girls always around, thinking you were older than you were. But you never had any use for them. This one is different, though. She's wearing your watch."

"It's complicated."

"It's always complicated." Tag grabs the bottle from Wes's hand. "So where'd you find her?"

Wes doesn't say anything, and Tag scowls. "Come on, man. Just tell me how you met her. She's clearly not one of us."

"She's not like anyone I've ever known."

"An easy life. It's written all over her."

"No." Wes's voice changes, hardens. "Not easy. Especially not since she met me."

Tag tilts his head as he studies him. "She's not here against her will, man. Anyone can see that. Girl's into you."

Wes looks down at the table. "I'm not good for her."

"You're trippin', man."

He is silent again, and Tag sets the bottle on the table with a dull thump. "What are you involved in anyway? What's got you running so scared?"

"Nothing."

"Ah, cut it out with that crap. You disappear for years and

then you come back all . . ." He makes a karate-chopping gesture.

Wes laughs a little. "What does that mean?"

"Like James Bond or something. You used to be clumsy. Always falling over shit. You couldn't fight to save your life. And now you're vaulting through windows like you're in some action movie. What happened to you?"

"I grew up. We both did."

Tag leans forward, until the outline of his body is close to Wes. "I know you wouldn't have left if you didn't have to. You weren't like the others. Did something . . . ?"

Wes shakes his head. "I'm sorry I left. But there's no mystery here. I was gone, I came back. That's all."

"Yeah, right." Tag takes a long swig from the bottle. When he drops it back down, he seems to have come to some kind of decision. "You know, Nikki and LJ weren't born on the streets like us. They weren't rich or anything, but they had a decent family. A mom. A dad. One day they came home and their parents were dead. Shot in the head, both of them. No one knows who did it. There was no money, no other relatives to take them on. They lost everything. Instead of going into the system and getting split up, they took off. Ended up on the streets. That was a few years ago."

Wes takes the bottle from Tag. "I don't see what this has to do with me."

"Chill out. I'm getting there. Now it's just Nikki and

Little J, but it wasn't always like that. They had a brother. He was about thirteen when they left home. I guess now he'd be sixteen, if he's still alive. One day they were out, trying to score some food. He ran ahead of them, turned a corner, and then he was gone. Disappeared without a trace, and they never saw him again. Just like you."

"I'm sitting right here, Tag. I didn't disappear."

"Yeah, but you're different. You're not street anymore. Something changed you."

"Kids disappear out here. You know that. Murders, drugs, juvie. It happens."

"All that stuff is messy. Court dates, blood. Not nothing." He sits back and watches Wes carefully. "There are rumors. About these men dressed in black snatching up kids. I want to know if that's what happened to you. I want to know if that's where Chris is."

"Chris?"

"Nikki's brother. She keeps searching, keeps believing that he's still out there. And now that I see you sitting across from me, I'm starting to wonder if he is."

Wes pushes away from the table and stands up. "Men in black? Vans? That's ridiculous. Stories people tell their kids to get them to behave."

"Wes." Tag stands too. He's so much shorter than Wes, but there's something about the way he carries himself that exudes confidence. "Tell me what you're hiding."

"Look, Tag. There's nothing going on. But . . ." He

hesitates, and I feel his gaze fall on me, a heavy weight. "If I am keeping something from you, it's for your own safety. Trust me on that."

Tag opens his mouth like he's going to say something else, but Wes cuts him off. "Tell Nikki her brother's dead. He might as well be."

Wes lies down on the floor next to the couch.

I close my eyes and listen as Tag shuts off the lamp and disappears into his bedroom.

Wes's breathing slows. I try to fall back asleep, but I can't.

The Montauk Project preys on orphans and street kids because they think no one will care about what happens to them. But Tag cared about losing Wes. Nikki and LJ cared about their brother, just like I care about my grandfather.

I flip over onto my back and stare up at the darkened ceiling. Grandpa was the one person in my life who was there whenever I needed him. When my parents were too busy with their own lives, he would make me dinner, help me with my homework, pick me up from school. And in five days, he'll disappear in this time line forever, another victim of the Montauk Project.

"What's wrong?" The whisper comes from the floor and I turn on my side. Wes is watching me. His face is in shadow, but I can see the dark shine of his eyes.

"I thought you were asleep."

"Your thinking woke me up."

"Funny."

I hear a rustling noise as he lifts up onto his elbow. "Tell me what's wrong."

I sigh. "I can't stop thinking about my grandfather."

"You want to help him."

"Whenever I close my eyes, I see him lying in the hospital bed screaming." My voice is hoarse, from sleep or grief, I don't know. "He's my grandfather. I can't leave him like that. I can't let them take him."

"I know you can't."

"I've been so afraid of messing up the time line again, but maybe that's the only way to make things right. Because this time line sucks, Wes."

He laughs shortly, a surprised sound. "Maybe it does. Changing time isn't always a bad thing, Lydia. The Project has stopped countless tragedies from happening over the years. It didn't work out for you in nineteen forty-four, but it could now." He waits a beat. "It's a gamble, though."

"I think it's worth taking. I won't let the Montauk Project have him." I shift until I'm almost hanging off the edge of the couch. "But what does that mean for you?"

"For the mission? As long as they can't trace any changes in the time line to me, I'll be okay."

"I don't want them to hurt you," I whisper.

"They won't. We'll be careful." He stares at me, unblinking. "I want to help you, Lydia. I don't want to send you back to a future you hate."

Send me back?

"What . . . what are you saying? I thought we were trying to get you out."

He is quiet for so long, I wonder if he fell asleep. When he finally speaks, his voice is lower. "What do you want, Lydia?"

I push my face into my elbow, and my hair falls thickly across my cheek. "I want a world where my grandfather is safe. Where I can have all the people I love in one place. Like my parents and Hannah and Mary, and . . ." I hesitate, but I'm tired of being so careful around him. "And you. I want to be with you."

"That's impossible," he says.

"Why?"

"Because those people exist in different times. In different *time lines*, even. Especially me."

I sit up fully and clasp my arms around my knees, squeezing tight. "I came here to find a way for us to be together. I thought it was what you wanted, too."

He sits up. "And have you? What's the secret solution to getting me free?"

I open my mouth, but no sound comes out.

"Exactly." His voice is a slash in the darkness. "Because there is no solution. You should forget about me, Lydia. Take me off the list of people you care about."

"But—"

He lies back down and turns away until he's facing the

opposite side of the room. "We'll finish this mission. You can visit Dean, and do what you need to do to save your grandfather. But after that . . ."

He trails off. After a minute, his body relaxes. It's a calculated move; he's not asleep, but he wants me to think he is.

I lie down on my side and stare at his back.

Sleep doesn't come. I stay frozen like that for a very long time.

In the morning, I wake as the sun is starting to stream in through cracks in the boards over the windows. I'm on my side, curled in a ball, and I slowly unfurl, stretching out my legs and arms.

And then I remember.

I glance over the side of the couch. Wes is lying on his stomach on the floor next to me, his left arm stretched to the side.

"He keeps moving around, like he's dreaming or something." I turn to see Nikki sitting at the table. She's dressed for the day, in a black dress and neon pink leggings. Her hair is up, blue streaks mixing with the brown in a messy ponytail.

"What time is it?" My voice is rough.

"Early. Just past dawn."

My stomach makes a gurgling noise and I press my hand to it. "Is there anything to eat?"

She shakes her head. "This isn't a hotel, Princess. There's

no breakfast unless I can scrounge something together before the boys wake up."

I should have realized, after how dinner arrived last night. "Are you going out to get food, then?"

She nods.

I think of the story Tag told Wes. Nikki might not be Little J's mom, but it's been her job to feed and clothe him for the past few years. While I was worrying about what to wear to my freshman formal, she was trying to keep her family together.

"I could come . . . help you. If you want." My voice is soft as I brace myself for her rejection.

She purses her lips. After a long minute, she shrugs. "I could care less." She gets up and walks over to the door. It opens with a low creaking sound. She pauses with her back to me. "So are you coming, or what?"

I look back down at Wes. It's probably not dangerous to be out in the city without him and after last night I think we both need some distance. Still, what will he think when he wakes to find me gone?

"Well?"

I get up from the couch, carefully stepping over Wes's prone form. "Yeah, I'm coming."

Even though it's early morning, the air is muggy, like a wet blanket that settles thick and heavy on our skin. Nikki and I turn onto Avenue C. The East Village is quiet and empty, with few cars passing and even fewer people on the street. I suppose even drug dealers have to sleep sometime.

Nikki walks quickly, her short legs swallowing up the sidewalk as fast as they can. I'm taller than her by a few inches, but I struggle to keep up. We're both quiet, and I try to think of something to say.

"I heard Tag talking about your brother Chris last night," I blurt out. "I'm sorry."

I wince as soon as the words leave my mouth, but Nikki just scowls and lifts one shoulder. "It is what it is."

I glance over at her. "Does that kind of thing happen a lot around here?"

"Kids disappearing? Yeah."

"Have you known others?"

She stops walking and puts one hand on her hip. "Why are you so interested in this?"

"I—"

"This is the ghetto, Princess. Kids disappear all the time. Most people don't care. Just let it go."

But I can't. "*I* care, and you do too. That counts for something."

"So what? It doesn't change anything."

I meet her eyes. "I guess I'm just curious why no one else notices or does anything about it."

"Some people notice." She starts walking again.

"What does that mean?"

She doesn't answer.

"I'm not the bad guy," I tell her. "I'm just trying to help."

She laughs. It's a cruel sound. "Are you going to swoop

in and fix everything? The little white girl princess come to rescue the poor street kids? Spare me."

My mouth falls open. "No. I—forget it."

We walk in silence for a minute. The worst part is that she's right—she has no reason to trust me. No reason to tell me anything.

I can't stop those kids from disappearing. No one can.

"I'm sorry," I say stiffly. "You're right, I should mind my own business."

She rolls her eyes. "Calm down, Princess. No offense, but I can tell that's not one of your strengths."

"Yeah, I guess not."

She grabs my arm and we both stop. Her voice is softer as she says, "Look, if you want to know more about this, you should talk to LJ, okay? He has a list."

"A list?"

"Of the kids who disappeared. He's been working on it for years."

"Why—"

But her fingers suddenly dig into my arm, and her brown eyes light up. "He's here. Come on." She tugs me down the sidewalk.

An hour later, we arrive back at the apartment carrying a bag of slightly bruised fruit.

"You found breakfast?" Tag comes out of his room. He stretches his arm over his head, and his shirt rises a little, showing the dark skin of his stomach. I was wrong before; he is attractive, even if he wouldn't be considered classically handsome. But his eyes are almost as dark as Wes's, and he has a strong, square jaw. "What'd you girls find out there?"

Nikki dumps the bag on the table and walks over to him. "Some fruit." Her words are muffled as she buries her face against his chest.

"Viktor again?"

Nikki nods, and her blue ponytail bobs up and down. "Princess here helped."

Tag catches my eye over her head. He looks surprised. "You the decoy?"

"I guess. Nikki just told me to go talk to some pervy guy selling fruit, and the next thing I knew she'd unloaded half his cart."

Tag laughs. "I would have liked to see that." He lets go of Nikki and reaches for the bag. "You got any bananas in there?"

LJ suddenly appears next to us, his hand closing over an orange. He moves so quietly that it takes me a minute to realize he's there.

Speaking of missing people. "Where's Wes?"

"He's in the bathroom," LJ replies.

I grab an apple and turn to leave the room.

"We had to talk him out of going after you." Tag's voice makes me pause near the door. "I convinced him that Nikki could take care of herself."

"So can I," I snap without turning around.

"Wes knows that. He said you were tough." Tag's voice becomes softer. "But he was pretty upset when he realized you weren't here."

I sigh and step into Tag's room.

The bathroom door is open and I see Wes inside, standing near the sink. He's bent over, his hands cupped around the chipped porcelain. He's gripping it so hard his knuckles have turned a sickly blue color, and he's shaking. His back, his arms, his legs. Every part of him trembles.

I stop in the middle of the bedroom. Wes doesn't even seem to notice me, which is alarming enough; he always seems to know when I'm in a room.

But not this time.

The shaking gets more violent, enough to rattle the sink against the wall. I start to wonder if he's having a seizure. I take a step closer.

His eyes cut to the side as he finally notices me. He stands up and his body stills. But the movement costs him—his face is pale white, and I can see the sweat gathering on the back of his neck.

"Wes." I move forward. "Are you okay? What was that?"

"Nothing." His voice is cracked and low. He clears his throat. "Nothing. I'm fine."

"Are you sure? It looked—"

"I'm fine, Lydia." He shouts the words, and I freeze, a few feet away from him. Just yesterday, I was thinking how natural he seemed to be in this squat, but now it is as though he is made of glass and any touch will shatter him.

There's a pause. Wes ignores me, staring down at his hands.

"Tell me what's going on," I finally say.

"Nothing. I was worried about you, that's all."

"I'm not the one shaking in a bathroom."

"It was nothing. Forget about it." He takes a deep breath, in and out, and then his shoulders fall and he steps forward. "We should go see McGregor before it gets too late."

I nod, still watching him carefully. Something is very, very wrong, but I know Wes well enough to know that he won't tell me. At least not until he's ready.

I press the red apple into his palms, where it looks smaller than it is, dwarfed by his large hands. "Eat this," I tell him, instead of what I'm really thinking. "You have to keep your strength up."

"Thanks."

He turns and walks from the room. I follow him, wishing I knew how to solve all of the problems we're facing. Even if I don't fully understand what they are.

CHAPTER 12

John McGregor? Hi, this is Sarah Bernstein from the *East Hampton Star.* We're interested in interviewing you about the upcoming election." I hold the pay phone as far away from my ear as I can. I thought the subway smelled like urine, but it has nothing on this phone booth. "I know this is unorthodox, to approach you directly, but since you're from Montauk I was wondering if you'd be willing to do a last-minute favor for a local paper?"

"Um . . . sure. That shouldn't be a problem." His voice sounds muffled in my ear. "When were you thinking?"

I look up at his building across the street. The glass walls of this booth are smudged, but I think I can still pinpoint the window to McGregor's apartment. "Would now be okay? I'm in the city with a colleague, and we're not far from your neighborhood."

"I . . . I guess that's fine. There's a diner near Battery Park called Timmy's Luncheonette. I could meet you there in half an hour."

"Great. See you soon." I hang up and step out of the booth. Wes is leaning against the glass, watching me closely.

"It worked?"

"I told you it would."

I adjust my dress and stare at my reflection in the window of a nearby deli. The lipstick Nikki let me borrow is starting to melt in the heat and I wipe away a smudge under my bottom lip.

Wes straightens. His hair is gelled again, and he's wearing the pinstriped shirt, though it is now wrinkled and a little stained. Hopefully McGregor won't examine us too carefully.

We're not carrying anything except for the newspaper clipping of Dean, tucked into Wes's pocket. He convinced me to leave the rest of my grandfather's files at the squat, telling me we wouldn't need the information and that Tag would keep it safe. It's a testament to how much Wes obviously trusts him.

"You ready?"

"Yep."

The clipped word makes Wes pause. "Lydia. About last night."

I refuse to look at him, instead walking down the sidewalk toward the neon green Luncheonette sign. "I don't care about last night." I stop and smooth my hands over my dress. "Okay, that's not true. I do. But I'm not going to fight you on it, Wes. I'll save my grandfather and go back to my own time." A passing businessman gives me a look, but I ignore him. "But . . . I just . . . want to know that you're okay. It's not only the shaking. You seem different. Something isn't right."

He runs his hand over his hair in a nervous gesture. "It was nothing. I'm the same."

I stare at him for a moment, but he won't meet my eyes. "Okay, Wes. Have it your way." I step forward, so that I'm no longer in his shadow. "Let's go meet McGregor."

The lighting in the diner is harsh, making the bags under John McGregor's eyes look deep and sallow. "I was surprised that the *Star* would have heard about this election." He turns a pink packet of Sweet'N Low over and over in his hands.

Only a counter separates the diner from the kitchen, and I can hear pans clanging and the sound of grease popping in the fryer. "We're always interested in locals who are doing amazing things," I say over the noise.

He shrugs. That defeated look has not left his eyes and he sits with his elbows slumped over the table. "I'm not sure how amazing this is."

"To be close to winning a city council election? That's quite an accomplishment!" I keep my voice light.

McGregor—or John, as he insisted we call him—doesn't answer.

"John?" I prod.

"What?" He jerks his head up. "I'm sorry. I've been out of it the past few days."

If John ever had a politician's charisma it is gone now, replaced with a melancholy sullenness. I glance over at Wes, but he is staring at the wall, seemingly lost in thought. It's like I'm the only person at the table who's even here.

"You seem a little distracted," I say to both of them pointedly.

Wes shoots me a look, but John just sighs. "I really am sorry. I had some distressing family news in the past few days. Maybe this isn't the best time to do this."

"If you don't mind me asking, are you all right?"

"I . . . yes." He looks up and attempts to smile. Even as I watch, it crumbles, falling away from his face. "No. I'm not." He drops his hands down onto the table, tossing the sugar packet aside. "I found out a relative of mine is . . . going through a rough time. It hasn't been easy."

"I'm really sorry." I reach across the table and squeeze his hand briefly. "That must be difficult. If you want to talk about it . . ."

He huffs and shakes his head. "You're a reporter. The last person I should be talking about my personal life with." But he is clearly itching to tell someone, because he leans forward slightly and drops his voice. "This is off the record, right?"

"Of course."

"A cousin of mine is in the psychiatric ward at Bellevue. It's hitting me harder than it should."

I make a sympathetic noise. "What happened?"

"I don't know." He sits back in the booth. He hasn't touched the coffee in front of him, but it's still hot and the steam curls up into the air between us. "We haven't spoken in years. A mutual acquaintance told me what happened to him. Apparently he went crazy. His family has stopped visiting him. It's a goddamn mess."

"I'm sorry." More than he knows; I hate the idea of my grandfather being alone with his own thoughts. My father must be so angry to abandon him in that place.

Wes shifts in his seat, and rests his hand next to mine on the table. I look at him out of the corner of my eye. He's staring down at our almost-touching hands, but at least he seems to be listening now.

"It's awful. I should have found out about it sooner. I should have done something. We grew up together. He always had these crazy ideas, but it was just part of who Peter was. To see him like this . . ." John rubs a hand over his mouth. He has two days' worth of stubble on his cheeks and chin.

"No one in your family told you about him before now?" I ask.

"I had a falling out with my father, and my mom died when I was a kid. I haven't even been back to Montauk since I left six years ago. God." He shakes his head. "Poor Peter."

"What was he like, when you saw him?"

"Delusional. Rambling. He gave me this computer disk, told me to give it to his family. I guess I should mail it, I don't know . . ."

I sit up a little. "A disk?"

"Yeah." John reaches into his jacket pocket and pulls out a black floppy disk. He slaps it down onto the linoleum table. "I've just been carrying it around with me."

I stop myself from reaching out to touch the square piece of plastic. "I could bring it back to Montauk for you, if you want. I'm headed there later."

He narrows his eyes. "You're a reporter. A stranger. I don't even know what's on here. I haven't had the chance to open it yet."

"I am a reporter, that's true," I say slowly. "But I'm also from Montauk, and that makes me a neighbor. You know what it's like to be a local out there. I'm not some cutthroat journalist. Please let me help." I give him my best trustworthy look. "I promise to keep this safe, and make sure it ends up in the hands of Peter's family."

He stares at me for a moment, then pushes the disk across the table toward me. "He's a Bentley. You can find his son at the local hardware store."

I close my fingers around the floppy disk. "I know where that is."

"Thank you." He smiles, and it's the first real one since he arrived. "I was dreading dealing with this. I'm not . . . ready to go back there yet."

"I understand."

He gets up from the table. "If you'll excuse me. I . . . I need to go. Feel free to contact my campaign manager about rescheduling that interview. And thanks again." He touches his forehead, then leaves the small diner.

"I think it's safe to say that your grandfather is responsible for McGregor losing focus," Wes says as soon as the door closes behind John.

"That's probably a safe bet." I hold up the disk. "What do you think is on this?"

"I don't know. Maybe something about 'the mark of the traveler?'" He turns to face me, none of that former detachment in his face. I frown. It's not like Wes to just drop out of a moment like that.

"You did a good job of convincing him to give it to you," Wes says.

"My journalistic powers at work. How are we going to open this? Do libraries in the eighties even have computers?" I shake the floppy disk. It's oddly flexible, which is apt, given its name. I've heard about these before, but I've never actually seen one in person.

"I don't think so. But there's one back at the squat."

I raise my eyebrows.

"It's in LJ's room," Wes continues. "Tag told me he built

it out of spare parts and stuff. Apparently he was really into computers before his parents were killed."

"Hopefully he'll let us use it. He seemed so shy yesterday." I slide out of the booth. "But first we need to stick to the plan and go find Dean. You're right; I can't put it off forever. We can deal with whatever's on this disk later tonight."

CHAPTER 13

Wes stares up at a large brick building that I immediately recognize from the newspaper clipping. "This is it. Seventy-ninth Street. You were right, it is a hotel."

"The Richardson," I read off the sign over the door. There's a red awning out front, but no sign of a doorman, and no sign of Dean.

"Are you ready?" Wes asks.

I watch the glass doors of the hotel closely, waiting for Dean to walk outside at any moment. The anticipation is a wild thing inside of me, clawing and pacing in my stomach.

"I think so."

It wasn't hard to find the building Dean was standing in front of in the photo. We took the subway up to the neighborhood mentioned in the article, the Upper West Side, near Riverside Park. The first deli owner we talked to recognized the hotel, and sent us here, to Seventy-ninth Street and West End Avenue.

Wes and I walk up the wide steps. There's no hotel staff outside, and I take a long, shallow breath. What if my grandfather was wrong, and it was just a Dean look-alike? What if it was him, but he's quit since then, lost somewhere in this huge city, in this unfamiliar time?

The closer we get to the elaborately decorated double doors, the more ridiculous it seems: my great-grandfather from the forties was sent through a faulty time machine and ended up stranded in 1989, working as a doorman? I almost grab Wes's arm, asking him to turn around, but we've come so far. I have to at least see what pushed my grandfather over the edge of sanity. I have to know if this person is really Dean.

We open the glass doors ourselves and enter a blue-and-gold lobby. A man is crossing the wide marble floor, coming right for us. He's dressed in a blue uniform, with a small cap on his head. As soon as I see his face, I *do* grab Wes's arm, but this time to steady myself. My grandfather wasn't crazy. This man is Dean Bentley.

"Can I help you?" Dean asks in his familiar voice. He's smiling broadly. He looks the same as he did in 1944, with heavy brows and military-short dark hair. "Sorry I wasn't at my post, but let me get your luggage while you check in to the hotel."

He gets a good look at our faces, and his smile fades. He recognizes us. "If you pardon me asking, you seem a little young to be checking in to a room by yourself. Are you staying with your parents today?"

"Dean." I choke on the word. "What are you doing here?"

"I'm sorry?" He looks confused; his brows furrow, causing sharp lines to appear on his forehead.

"It's me. Lydia." I feel tears gather in my eyes and I blink as Dean's features blur. I never thought I'd see him again. I thought I was responsible for *killing* him. And here he is, standing right in front of me. "I can't believe it's you."

"Lydia?"

I nod, and reach out my hands. "It's me. I came here to . . . well, it's a long story."

"I don't think I follow."

I look into his face and see that he's still confused. Is he just surprised that I'm in this time period? Is he afraid that the Project might be watching? I glance around the room and then lean in closer to him.

"It's *me*. Lydia," I whisper. "Your great-granddaughter."

The man looks shocked, and then begins to laugh. The sound hits me right in the chest. Dean's voice. His laugh. I never thought I'd hear it again. It makes me think of Mary, Lucas, and the Bentleys. I miss them so much, and I'll most likely never see any of them again.

But here's Dean. One small piece of that life I haven't lost.

His voice cuts through my thoughts. "Do I look old enough to have a great-granddaughter?"

He doesn't. It's as though no time has passed, and he was never betrayed by the very Project he helped to build. As though Dr. Faust never threw him, broken and bleeding, into the time machine. I want to fling my arms around him, but his words begin to chip away at the joy that has been bubbling inside of me.

"It's me. Lydia."

He shakes his head. "Sorry, I've never met a Lydia before."

I look around the lobby again. Is it not safe? Are there people watching us even now? "Dean, I realize this might not be the best place to talk. We need to go somewhere private. I need to know how you survived the TM and how long you've been in this time period."

His gaze becomes wary. "What's a TM? I don't know what you're talking about. I'm sorry, but this conversation is starting to make me uncomfortable. I think you've confused me with someone else."

"Lydia." Wes is watching the people nearby. The lobby isn't packed, but there are several guests standing next to the check-in counters, and a few of them are watching us. "We shouldn't do this here."

"Do you know someplace safe where we can talk?" I ask Dean, keeping my voice low.

"I don't think that's necessary." His gaze shifts to

somewhere over my shoulder, as though he's looking for an escape. "If you'll excuse me."

He steps to the side, trying to skirt us. But I step with him. "What is going on?" I whisper. "Can you not talk here? Is it not secure?"

"I really don't know what you're talking about. I'm sorry." He sounds so serious. I scan his face, trying to read behind his words.

"What's going on?" I repeat.

He frowns. There are thick lines bracketing his mouth that I never noticed before. "I'd like to know that too."

I stare up at him. His green eyes—so much like my own, so much like my *grandfather's*—are cold, and . . . indifferent. There's not even a hint of recognition. After Wes, I've become somewhat of an expert on people who hide their emotions, but this is different. He's not hiding anything, because there's nothing left to hide.

Unless Dean is the world's best actor—which I know he isn't—then he honestly has no idea who I am.

"Oh my god. You look like Dean, you sound like him, but you're not him, are you? You don't remember anything."

"What?" Both Dean and Wes look confused.

I clench my fists and try one more time. "Dean Bentley. That's your name. You're the son of Harriet and Jacob. Married to Elizabeth. Doesn't any of this sound familiar? Try to remember," I plead.

His frown deepens. "I am married. But my wife's name

is Theresa. Not Elizabeth."

"What?" I press my hand to my chest. I feel the hard metal of Wes's watch shift under my fingertips. "You're married to someone here? In this time period? Did they make you marry her? Did they make you forget your old life?"

He bristles. "I've been a happily married man for two years, and no one makes me do anything. Except maybe my wife. Now if you'll excuse me."

"Wait. Please. I don't understand. How can you not remember any of it? Not the Project? Not Eliza?" I feel tears form again, and I dig my fingernails into my palms, trying to use the pain of it to distract me.

"Lydia." Wes touches my shoulder, but I ignore him, concentrating on Dean.

"What did they do to you? Please, you have to remember."

I don't even notice as an older man in a plain brown suit approaches. He extends his hand toward Wes, who takes it reluctantly. "Mr. Turner, general manager of the hotel. Is there a problem here?"

"No, sir." Dean smiles pleasantly at the older man. "These two thought I was someone else. They've realized their mistake, and they're leaving now."

Mr. Turner looks Wes and me over. "Not the first time this has happened to you, is it, Frank? You must have a twin out there."

I wipe at the tears on my cheeks, trying to hide how upset I am. "Was someone else here looking for Dean?"

"Dean?" Mr. Turner laughs. It's a booming sound, and

more of the people in the lobby turn to stare at us. "There was an older man who came around a few months back. We had to have security throw him out. Kept coming back and just sitting across the street, accosting Frank whenever his shift was over. People like that shouldn't be allowed to roam the streets. They're like wild dogs." He smiles at us. "Strange coincidence, you two showing up and asking the same questions. I don't need to call security again, now do I?"

"No." Wes gently takes my arm. "We're going."

I let Wes lead me forward. We're almost to the door when I stop. I can't leave it like this. *I can't.*

I yank away from Wes's hold and spin around. Dean and Mr. Turner are still standing in the middle of the lobby watching us go. "What about your son?" I yell. "What about Peter? How could you forget Peter?"

Something flickers in Dean's long, thin face, and I freeze. He remembers. But then whatever it is disappears, and he just stares at me, as blank as an empty canvas.

"You're mistaken," he says calmly. "I have no son."

Wes and I leave the hotel. The tears are streaming down my face now, but I let them fall, making no move to wipe them away. Wes links his arm through mine, as though he's some old-fashioned suitor, and leads me down the street. We walk in the opposite direction of the subway, toward a narrow, steep stretch of green grass. As we get closer, I realize that it's a park built into the side of a hill. A jogger passes us and sees my face. He averts his eyes and keeps running, head down. A city person, used to ignoring something that makes them uncomfortable.

We sit down on a bench next to a cement pathway that winds through the park. Below us, a highway runs alongside the grass. I hear cars passing, a steady rushing noise that ebbs and flows like the waves of an ocean. It reminds me of Montauk, of home, and the thought of it causes a sharp pain to settle in the center of my chest.

"It's like he's a different person," I say to Wes after a minute. My voice sounds high and nasal and I sniff loudly. The tears have finally stopped, but my nose is stuffed and I have that tender, sore feeling you get after crying. "Like they erased his mind."

Wes reaches into the pocket of his slacks and pulls out a tissue. "Here." He hands it to me.

It's wadded up and torn, but I take it anyway and blow my nose. "Do you think that's even possible?"

He leans forward, his elbows resting on his spread-apart knees. The pose somehow makes his body look longer, even though he's bent almost in half. "I think anything's possible when it comes to the Project."

"He has amnesia or something. Maybe from the machine. Maybe they did it to him. But I looked into his eyes, Wes. He was gone. There was an emptiness I've never seen before."

Wes is silent. I feel curiously empty too, hollowed out

and no longer whole. "I wonder if Dean is still in there somewhere," I say.

"If it was because of the Project, then probably not."

I see Wes's shadow spread out across the pavement in front of us. The way he's sitting makes the dark pattern on the ground look like some kind of beast with long arms and no head. Mine just looks like a girl with her head tilted down. I move a little, scooting closer to Wes. We're not touching, but our shadows merge together in a distorted blob until we're one giant monster.

"It would make sense for them to experiment with erasing memories," I say, thinking out loud. "If people can't remember something, then they can't talk about it."

Wes frowns. "I doubt he got amnesia from the machine. They wouldn't have let him reenter society if that was the case. They would have just killed him."

"Couldn't he be lying to us about his memories? Maybe he escaped and now he's working here, trying to hide from the Project. He could have been worried that we'd blow his cover." I can't keep the hope out of my voice even though I know it's a long shot—I saw Dean standing in that lobby. He was like a marionette or something. Dead-eyed but still putting on a show. And it's not hard to imagine who's holding the strings.

"I don't think so," Wes answers. "I've gotten pretty good at knowing if someone's lying. He wasn't. Somehow he's forgotten his entire life in nineteen forty-four."

I grit my teeth together at the thought of what Dean

probably endured. "I bet he's their guinea pig. Erase his mind, reenter him into society, and see what happens. Do you think he's even really married? Does his 'wife' know he really loves Eliza? And his son?"

Wes is silent.

"I have to get him out of there." I push my bangs away from my forehead impatiently. "I have to rescue him from this."

Wes still doesn't speak, but I feel the tension coming off him. "What?" I turn on my hip until I'm facing him on the bench. "You don't agree?"

He hesitates.

"Just spit it out, Wes."

"I think . . . that you should be cautious. He might not want to be rescued."

"He doesn't *know* he wants to be rescued."

"Lydia." Wes sits back and studies me. "If we're right, then he doesn't remember anything. And he never will again. Those memories have been wiped clean. It's not like they're saved in some container or something." He doesn't touch my knee again, but his hand hovers over it, and I can feel the heat from his skin even through the fabric of my dress. "We can't go barreling in there to save a man who doesn't care if he's saved or not. We'd be destroying whatever life he has left."

I want to scream at him, to beat the metal bench with my fists, but I force myself to consider his words. Dean is not the person I remember. Maybe he's even happy now, with this Theresa woman. Do I have the right to take that away from him? To uproot his new life, put him into a dangerous situation he might not survive in order to send him back to a world he doesn't even remember? What's the point?

I think of the last time I tried to save Dean, and what the consequences were. I changed time, and destroyed three—or more—lives in the process. I have to stop trying to play God in these situations, thinking I know more than everyone else. Thinking that my own pursuit of the truth is just as important to other people as it is to me. Dean doesn't *care* about the truth. At least not anymore.

"I can't believe this is how it ends for him. A doorman in a hotel in nineteen eighty-nine. His family never knowing what happened to him."

Wes touches my knee lightly, just for a second. "You'll know the truth. That's important to you—solving the mystery, even if you don't like what you find."

I smile, even though I'm struggling not to cry again. "You think you know me so well, don't you?"

He gives me a sort of smirking smile. "I think I know you a little bit."

I close my eyes and feel the afternoon sun burn against the delicate skin of my eyelids.

For the second time in six weeks, I am forced to leave Dean to his fate.

CHAPTER 14

The sky is turning twilight gray. We've been sitting on this bench for hours, just listening to the cars below and watching the Hudson River, which spreads out beyond the highway—the slow-moving boats, the bridges that spark silver in the sunlight, and the green cliffs that make up the shoreline of New Jersey.

I haven't wanted to move, because I know that the minute I do everything becomes real again and I have to accept the choice that I've made. Wes seems to sense this, and he sits quietly next to me. Not talking, but just . . . there.

"We should go back to the squat," I finally say. From somewhere in the park I hear the sound of a child shrieking. I can't tell if it's laughter or fear. "I need to open that disk. It's the only lead I have left for discovering why my grandfather disappears. Dean is certainly a dead end."

Wes doesn't say anything. He appears to be thinking about something hard, though I'm not sure what it is.

"Are you ready to go?" I ask.

"I have a better idea." He abruptly takes my hand and pulls me up from the bench. He moves quickly down the concrete path of the park, and I struggle to keep up with him.

"Wes, what—"

Up ahead, I see a playground tucked into the trees. It has a large jungle gym, a set of rusted swings, and a fountain in the middle. Even though it's late and the park is empty, the sprinklers are still on. The water sprays everywhere, shooting high up into the air and bouncing off of the concrete ground.

Wes tugs me forward, leading us into the gated area. "The disk!" I shout, and I have just a second to toss it onto a bench before Wes picks me up by the waist and spins us both into the falling water.

I shriek as it soaks through the fabric of my dress. It is freezing cold, but the city air is hot and stale, and so I raise my hands up high, feeling the water glide down my skin.

Wes sets me on the ground. His hair is plastered to his forehead, and I smile up at him through the drops of water that cling to my eyelashes. He smiles back and reaches for me, but I turn on my heel and run toward the jungle gym. I can hear him chasing me as I leave the fountain behind.

I am almost to the tall wooden structure when he catches me, sliding his arm around my waist again and spinning me in a circle.

We are both laughing when he finally lets go of me. I pull my dress away from my body. It is soaked through.

Wes moves to stand in front of me. "Better?" he whispers, pushing my wet, tangled hair away from my cheeks.

"Lots," I reply. He grins at me. The energy coming from him is so strong that he seems to be vibrating with it. He flings back his hair and uses both hands to push it away from his face, and I look at him more closely. There is something . . . off about his features. His mouth is too wide; his eyes are too bright. My smile fades, but he doesn't notice.

"Wes," I say slowly. "Are you feeling okay?"

"I feel great. Alive." He looks down at me. His movements are jerky, so different from his usual grace. "Want to stay here for a while?"

I push away the feeling of dread that's growing inside of me. "Yeah. I do." Maybe this is just Wes's way of learning how to open himself up to another person. There's bound to be a little awkwardness in the beginning. I'm probably worrying for nothing. But the image of his shaking against the chipped sink flashes through my head.

"Come on," Wes says. He leads me back toward the water. It feels colder this time, on the bare skin of my arms, and I shiver under the falling stream.

When we get back to the squat, my dress is still damp, clinging to my body. I'm hoping that Nikki has something I can borrow, but we find the apartment empty and dark. I turn on one of the floor lamps, and a glow spreads through the open space.

Wes walks across the room to the window. I think about him standing in the falling water, his light-colored shirt molded to the outline of his chest.

He turns his head to catch me looking at him and we both freeze.

"We should open up that disk." My voice is a whisper.

He nods, but his gaze drops to the pale column of my neck. To my collarbone. To his pocket watch, against my chest.

I swallow hard.

"Ahem." The noise is quiet, but we both hear it. Wes looks up, staring at something past my head. I spin around. LJ is standing in his bedroom doorway, his face on fire.

"When did you get here?" Wes demands.

"I, um . . ." LJ blushes even more, though I'm not sure how it's physically possible. "I was here the whole time. In there." He points behind him, toward his room. His body is holding the sheet back from the doorway, and I can see the harsh light from his computer monitor.

Wes opens his mouth, then closes it. He's clearly shaken; it's not like him to be unaware of someone's presence when they're that close, even if they are as quiet as LJ.

Wes is many things, but easily fazed is not one of them. I take a small step toward him.

"I, sorry, I didn't mean to . . . you know." LJ moves his hands awkwardly in front of his body.

"It's fine," I say. "We had a question for you anyway. Could we borrow your computer for a minute?"

"Sure. But, um . . . there's something I think I should tell you."

"What is it?" Wes sounds impatient, which also isn't like him; he must be really rattled.

LJ's face falls, and his large brown eyes make him look like a kitten that just got kicked. "I uh, did something that you might not like. I think you two need to know about it."

I tilt my head, watching him carefully. "What did you do?"

He bites his lip, hesitating. Then his brow furrows and he stands up a little taller. "It's in here."

Wes and I exchange a glance before following him.

The bedroom is small, with two mattresses lying on the ground and a sliver of a window. A makeshift desk dominates the back wall, made of plywood and milk crates. LJ's computer rests on top in a tangle of wires. It is clunky and overly large, with a dull, black screen.

LJ stands over his monitor, his back to both of us. "Tag asked me to keep an eye on that stuff you left here. And, um . . . I looked inside."

I feel a twinge of panic, and I turn to stare at Wes. Tag was supposed to keep the information on my grandfather safe.

What did LJ do?

Unaware of our reaction, or maybe hiding from it, he sits down at the desk and starts to type something. The computer screen in front of him is black, with a bright blue cursor that blinks at the top of the page. "Those letters and numbers that were written in that book, *The Metamorphosis*, I recognized them." He says the words slightly robotically, and I realize he's only half paying attention to us. Funny how he forgets to be embarrassed when he's caught up in his digital world.

Wes's cheekbones are more pronounced, like he's gritting his teeth together hard. "So you're saying that you stole our personal property when you knew we didn't want anyone to find it." His voice is deceptively calm, and the sound of it breaks through the computer spell around LJ. He turns to look up at Wes, but when he sees his face, he cowers back down in his seat.

"I'm sorry," he whispers. "But I found something I think you'll want to see."

"What was there to find?" My voice isn't much friendlier than Wes's was, but maybe LJ found something we can use. "Wes and I thought they were just a random pattern."

"But they're not." Despite the glacial freeze emanating from Wes, LJ is beginning to sound excited. "They don't make much sense the way they're written, it's true. But then I realized they weren't just letters, they were elements, and it all came together."

"Elements?" Wes sounds curious, though the coldness never leaves his tone.

LJ ducks a little lower, but his excitement is clearly outweighing his self-preservation. "It looks like nonsense, but when you arrange it in a different way . . ." He holds out a sheet of scribbled-on paper, and Wes peers at it.

"It's a molecular formula," Wes finishes.

"A what?" I lean over Wes's arm, and see: $SO_4N_2H_{11}C_9$-O-$C_9H_{11}N_2O_4S$. I remember seeing formulas like that in chemistry class.

"It's a serum of sorts. It looks like it could be a type of medicine or something." LJ drops the paper back down on his desk. "The strain isn't that far from the makeup of penicillin. That's how I recognized some of the numbers in the first place."

"Why did you do this? Why do you care?" Now Wes sounds suspicious, and I tense. I feel like I should be prepared for something, though I'm not sure what it is. But if Wes thinks that LJ might be involved with the Project, then we have a huge problem on our hands.

"I like solving problems. Stuff like this makes sense to me." He sees our expressions and sinks down again. "I was just curious. I'm really sorry I went through your stuff, but I thought you would want to know what it meant. That's all."

I don't know why, but I believe him: the only time LJ seems to come out of his shell is when he's talking about codes and computers. It's easy to believe that he saw a problem in front of him and he ignored our privacy in order to solve it.

"Okay," I say, "but what does—"

I stop speaking as the computer screen lights up. Words appear on the screen in a steady stream of blue light.

For Lydia.

"Did you just type that?" I ask LJ.

"No." LJ's eyes are glued to the blue light. "I'm in a chat room with this guy. He's sending it."

I suddenly feel cold. "What guy? Why does he know my name?"

"I don't know. He calls himself Resister."

"Resister?" I look at Wes with wild eyes. "I met someone with that same handle back in Montauk. He told me he was on the conspiracy message boards. He said he was working on a rebellion to take down the Project."

Wes takes a step toward me. "When was this?"

I quickly tell him about the man who came into my father's store back in 2012. I don't know why I didn't mention it before; I must have gotten so caught up in my grandfather, Dean, and McGregor that I forgot all about it. "But the man was in his thirties, Wes. If he was sending it from this time period, he would be . . ."

"A teenager," Wes finishes.

"What are you talking about?" LJ glances between the two of us. But before I can come up with some kind of explanation, more text appears on the screen. It is a replica of the exact molecular formula that LJ discovered in *The Metamorphosis.*

"How does he know this?" I whisper.

"What kind of chat room are you in right now?" Wes demands of LJ. "What do you know about this Resister?"

"We have a number we all dial into with our modems. It's secure." LJ's voice sounds higher. "The Resister set it up. We talk about conspiracy stuff. To try and find out why—"

"Kids are going missing," I cut in. "Nikki told me you've been looking into it. She said you have a list."

LJ opens one of his desk drawers and pulls out a hand-written list. There are about ten names on it. "Tag helped me with the names. The Resister said it's happening because of this conspiracy in an old army base on Long Island."

I suck in a breath.

Wes steps forward. "This guy shouldn't know Lydia's name. And he shouldn't know this formula you just figured out. Are you lying to us?"

"No, no, I swear!" LJ puts his hands up. "He's never mentioned this stuff before. He was just talking to me about Chris. He said he thinks he's probably still alive! I wanted to . . . believe him."

The screen blinks again. Blue writing appears: *The Mark of the Traveler.*

All of the tiny hairs rise on my arms. I bend over LJ's shoulder and type out: *How do you know this?*

But a blue line of text pops up: *Resister has left the room.*

"Can you hack into his server?" Wes asks. "Can you follow him?"

LJ shakes his head. "He's the one who set it up. He's hiding behind firewalls. I know how to hack, but not like that. . . ." He starts to pop his knuckles. Slowly and loudly, over and over. I ignore the sound as I try to process what's happening. The mark of the traveler? I had never heard that phrase before my grandfather screamed it at me yesterday. And why does this person—who's only a teenager now—know my name?

"Could this be coming from the future?" I whisper the words.

"I don't think that's possible," Wes says.

But LJ just looks at me. "I don't know what you're talking about, but this guy has built a kind of system I've never seen before. I've been in and out of chat rooms for years, but none with firewall protection like this."

"Jesus," Wes breathes. "Maybe it's coming from the Project."

LJ turns to face us. "What Project?"

"This is not some random message," I say to Wes. "Someone knew we would be here in this exact spot at this exact time. They wanted me to find it."

"Why you?"

"I don't know. Because I've already met him?" I rub my hand against my forehead. "He was talking about a rebellion. I wonder if this has to do with it?"

"Whatever it is, it's connected back to your grandfather."

"The disk." I look up. "I think we need to see what's on it."

Wes takes it from his pocket and hands it to a pale LJ. "Open this for us."

LJ looks confused, but slips it into his disk drive anyway. A folder pops up and he clicks on it.

A text-based document opens. Page after page of information appears. There are two words near the top: *The List*.

LJ scrolls down. It is a list of names and next to each is a brief description and then a set of numbers. It takes me a minute to realize that the numbers are actually dates, and there are always at least two of them. Sometimes three.

He keeps moving through the names. But then he stops. "Lydia . . ."

"Oh my god," I whisper. Because there, in neat black letters, is my own name.

CHAPTER 15

Lydia Katherine Bentley: great-granddaughter of Dean Patrick Bentley. Montauk, New York, I: April 4, 1995. Montauk, New York, D: July 30, 2012.

Wes grabs my shoulder and squeezes hard.

"The first date is my birthday. But what does the other one mean? Could it . . ." I pause. "Is it when I die?"

Wes's grip has become almost painful, biting into my skin. "No one can know that. Don't panic. We'll figure this out."

"Okay, okay."

His hand slides down my upper arm. He's almost touching the small raised scar on my skin. It's the same scar that matches his.

Something impossible starts to turn over in my head.

"LJ, let me see your list." My voice sounds like it's coming from far away.

He hands it to me, and moves away from the computer so I can sit down. I match up some of the names. Timothy Martinez. Alisha Parks. They're all on both lists. By the time I'm done checking, my fingers are shaking.

"Wes . . . is your name here too?"

Seeing my expression, he walks to the computer and leans over me. He taps down until he reaches the Ws. There are a hundred names, but no Wes. "Every person has a middle and a last name listed too," he says softly.

"And you don't know what yours is." I think of his pocket watch, and the initials etched into the side. It's a long shot, but I hold the watch up anyway and read the inscription again: *With love, WLE.* "Try the Es. See if there's a Wes or Wesley as a first name."

He scrolls quickly through the names. "Wait, stop." I slide my finger across the screen. The static on the glass crackles against my skin. "Wesley Benjamin Elliot."

Parents: Jane Marie Simmons and Lawrence Jonathan Elliot, both deceased. New York, New York, I: January 18, 1984, D: January 18, 1984.

"Does that date mean anything to you?"

He answers without looking at me. "It's the date I was taken by the Project."

"This is a list of people who have been disappeared." I can't keep the horror out of my voice.

"You don't know that."

"All the names match up."

"But what do these dates and random letters mean?"

"My *I* date is my birthday. But yours is the same as when you were taken, so it can't mean our births." I think out loud. "Maybe—"

I feel LJ grab my arm and I turn my head, suddenly realizing how much we've revealed.

"There's an explanation for this." I am ready to do damage control, though I have no idea how to explain away everything he just heard.

But LJ's mouth is open as he points at two entries not far above Wes's name. "Christopher Enriquez and Jesse Enriquez."

I look up at him. "Do those names mean something to you?"

"That's me. And my older brother, Chris." He lets go of me and takes a step backward. "Why is my name on this list? Why is yours? What's going on?"

But Wes is back to ignoring him. "Lydia, look at the dates."

I stare at the top name.

Christopher Jonathan Enriquez: son of Juan Franklin Enriquez and Judith Nicola Enriquez [terminated March 15, 1986.] Queens, New York, I: June 6, 1973. New York, New York, D: September 21, 1986.

I turn to LJ. "Is June sixth his birthday?"

His olive skin is chalky and his eyes are wide, making

him look like a little kid. "What's going on? What is this?"

I get up from the computer, taking a step toward him. "LJ," I say sharply. "Are those dates significant?"

At my voice he shudders a bit and visibly regroups. "The first date is Chris's birthday, and . . ."

"The second date is when he disappeared," Wes cuts in quickly. "Tag says he was about thirteen when it happened."

"And the dates for you? Is October third, nineteen seventy-five your birthday?"

"Yeah, yeah." LJ nods frantically. "It is."

"The second date is September sixteenth, nineteen eighty-nine," Wes tells me.

"That's in one month." I stalk across the small room, then back again, repeating the same steps over and over. "The second date is when everyone's taken. The *D* before it could stand for 'detained.'" I fight the nausea that's rising in my throat. "It means they're planning on coming for me."

Wes abruptly straightens from the computer. His eyes are narrowed. "No. They can't take you. Not after what we went through to keep you a secret from them."

"Maybe it wasn't enough?"

He grabs my hands, forcing me to stop pacing the room like some kind of caged animal. "It *was* enough. We didn't cause this."

"But . . ." I hesitate, thinking of the scar under my skin, of my grandfather screaming at me. "Wes, when did you get the scar on your arm?"

He gives me a strange look. "What?"

"The scar on your upper arm. When did you get it? Do you remember?"

"No. It was some time after they brought me in, though. I didn't have it as a kid. Lydia, what does that have to do with this list?"

The half-formed idea is still taking shape in my brain, and I'm afraid to say it out loud, afraid that it will sound ridiculous. Or, even worse, that it might be true.

But it's not in my nature to hide from the truth, and I square my shoulders and face Wes. "I have a theory about what the first date means."

He's working his jaw back and forth, so tightly that I'm worried he'll grind his teeth down into nothing. "Tell me."

I pry my hands out of his and then grab his wrist. "Remember what my grandfather said? About 'the mark of the traveler'? It was after he saw this." I lift Wes's wrist and place his hand just below my shoulder. "We have the same scar, Wes." I look at the monitor, at the mysterious list, a never-ending litany of names.

Wes frowns. "You think the first date has to do with this scar? How?"

I let go of Wes's hand and it falls limply to his side. "I think it's the date the person was scarred. Mine must have happened on my birthday; I've had this scar my whole life. Chris and LJ probably got it when they were born too. You got yours when you were taken in. It's why the two dates on your entry are the same."

Wes suddenly turns to LJ, who's watching us with wide eyes. "Let me see your arm."

LJ steps forward. He's clearly scared, but he pulls up his sleeve anyway. There, on his upper arm, is a slightly raised, circular scar. "He has it." My stomach falls. "This has to be 'the mark of the traveler' my grandfather was ranting about. We've been tagged, or something. Like animals. And this is some kind of master list, keeping track of when they . . . pick us, and when they actually bring us in."

"Lydia." Wes's voice is low. "If you're right, that means you'll be a recruit. You'll be brought into the Project."

But it's more than that. If I was tagged when I was a baby, then I was *always* destined to become a recruit. Everything we did to keep my involvement a secret was pointless; all of the sacrifices that Wes made for me meant nothing. Becoming a recruit is my fate.

I suddenly feel faint, like all the blood has rushed from my head, and I bend over, putting my hands on the edge of the desk. I sense rather than see Wes move closer to me. "I won't let them take you." He growls the words. "You won't become like me."

"Wes." I straighten and then fall into him. His hands curl around my back, and he holds me so tight it's as though he's trying to fuse my body into his.

"I don't mean to interrupt," LJ's voice still has that confused, panicked quality to is. "But can you please tell me what's going on?"

I pull away from Wes and we share a long glance. Finally, he nods slightly. I know we're both thinking the same thing: LJ has a right to know what's coming for him.

"You might want to sit down," I say, and he sinks into his desk chair. When I finish telling him about the Montauk Project and the recruits, he is white and shaking.

"Are you okay?" I kneel down in front of his chair.

He nods slowly. "It's almost a relief, I guess, to know what finally happened to Chris. To know that he's still alive, even if . . ."

I squeeze LJ's knee. "We have an advantage," I say quietly. "Because we know when they're coming. It means we can protect ourselves."

He nods slowly. I watch as his face changes, his eyes getting brighter. "We're forgetting something."

"What is it?" I stand up again.

He spins around to face the desk and picks up the sheet of paper he scribbled on earlier. "This. The serum. How does it fit in?"

"You said it was like a medicine," Wes says.

"Yeah, and the Resister sent us the same exact formula. It must be connected." Most people would have fallen apart at the news that a secret government conspiracy was after them, but LJ just hunches over the numbers, staring down at his paper with wide eyes.

I look over his shoulder. The letters and numbers blur together. "He sent it to me. He wanted me to put it together.

The serum has to be a part of the mark of the traveler."

LJ looks up at the computer and rereads the entry on himself, his voice only slightly faltering. "You said the *D* could stand for 'detained.' But what does the *I* stand for?"

I turn to Wes. "You have no memory of getting the scar?"

"No." His voice has changed; it sounds deeper than normal. "But that first day was a haze. I spent most of it drugged or unconscious."

LJ starts popping his knuckles again. A low, hollow sound.

"So we have a scar, and a serum that looks like a medicine." I push my bangs away from my forehead. The room is hot, stifling almost, and sweat gathers on my skin in tiny beads. "What if it's related? What if we were injected with the serum for some reason and that created that scar?"

LJ nods. "The *I* could stand for 'injection.'"

"Or 'inoculation,'" I say. "Like against a virus."

I look at Wes to see his reaction. He is staring down at the rough surface of the desk. I realize it has been several minutes since he last moved.

"What do you think?" I ask him gently.

No response. I step toward him but stop when his hand spasms against his side. He immediately balls his fingers into a fist.

"Wes? Are you okay?" I touch his arm lightly.

He turns to me, and I take a step back at the look on his

face. "How can you ask me if I'm okay when you're the one who just received a death warrant?"

"I'm not—"

"You always have to play the detective, don't you?"

My mouth falls open. Why is he angry with *me*?

"Are you sure we can trust this Resister person?" LJ asks tentatively.

"No," I tell him. "But he's clearly trying to tell me something. And it adds up, especially since I met him in the future. I think he wants me to help him with his rebellion."

LJ looks confused. "Even if you're in the past?"

I shrug.

"It's possible that someone is trying to mess with you," Wes snaps.

"We got the disk from my grandfather. We weren't even supposed to have it. All this Resister did was help us make the connection between the serum and the mark."

"He could be working for the Project. This all could have been orchestrated to make you fear them. To put you on edge."

"They aren't even supposed to know about me, remember? It doesn't make sense that I'd be a target."

Wes doesn't answer.

I feel like I can't breathe, but I force the words out anyway. "Well, I guess we'll know after I get kidnapped."

Wes scowls. "Don't say that."

"It's true, isn't it?"

"Even if it is, the date is in the future. Twenty years from now."

"So I go home, then get taken. Why should I even bother trying to get back to my own time period? I should just turn myself in to them now. Or hide out in the eighties for the rest of my life, praying they don't find out I'm here."

His eyes darken until they're almost black. "Stop talking like that. You don't know what this means. This is just some random theory you have. It could be nothing."

We square off, a few feet separating us. LJ backs away, moving closer to his computer and farther from us.

"It's a plausible theory, you know it is," I say. "You just don't want me to be right."

"Why are you so ready to believe this?"

"What choice do I have? We *have* to believe that this list is real. If we don't, something might happen to me or to LJ."

He takes a step toward me. "I won't let anything happen to you."

"How will you stop it?"

"I don't know!" He shouts the words and I freeze.

"Guys . . ."

I tear away from Wes's gaze and turn to LJ.

"What?" The word comes out shorter than I mean it to.

Wes spins around until his back is to me. I see his shoulders rise and fall quickly.

"This name. I know this girl." LJ points at someone on

the list. "Maria Hernandez. She lives in a squat down the street."

"LJ, I think you'll know a lot of the names on that list," I reply softly.

He makes a frustrated sound. "No, look at the date she's taken. August tenth, nineteen eighty-nine. That's today."

My heart sinks. "That means she's probably already gone."

He turns wet eyes up at me. "She's fourteen, Lydia. She's . . . I can't let them take her too."

I stare at him for a minute, then sigh. "Okay. Okay. What do you want to do?"

He looks down at the battered plastic watch on his wrist. "It's almost nine. She deejays at a club a few blocks from here. If they haven't gotten her already, that's where she'll be."

"So let's go."

He gives me a grateful look and stands up from his desk.

I hear the front door open. The three of us all turn toward the sound. "Hey!" Tag's voice calls out. "Anyone around?"

I reach out and grab LJ's arm. We're about the same height, and I lean in close to his ear. "You cannot tell anyone about this," I hiss. "Not Tag. Not Nikki. No one. Ever. You'd be putting them and yourself in danger. Promise me."

He nods curtly.

Tag pulls back the curtain and pauses in the doorway.

"Whoa." He takes in the tension coming off of us. "What's going on in here?"

I force myself to relax and smile at him. "Nothing. We were just talking about tonight."

LJ clears his throat. "We're going to Sinners."

"Cool, I'll tell Nikki. She'll want to come."

"We should go now," LJ says quickly. "I'm supposed to meet someone."

Tag holds back the curtain and makes an elaborate gesture with his hand. LJ smiles tightly and walks into the main room. Wes and I follow.

Nikki is standing near the dining-room table. "So, Sinners? Who are you trying to kid?" She gives LJ a look. "We all know why you want to go. Maria's the deejay tonight, huh?"

LJ visibly swallows. "Yeah. I hope so."

"Okay. Well, just let me get changed. I'll be two seconds." Her gaze travels over me. "Lydia, you better come with me. You can't wear that yuppie dress. I'll give you some jeans."

"We need to be quick," I say when I see LJ's pleading eyes. "Really quick."

Tag laughs. "Yeah right. I'd like to see that." He turns to Wes. "You need a clean shirt or something?"

Wes is silent.

He had been staring down at the floor, but he suddenly lifts his head. His eyes find mine immediately. His face is still cold and hard, though there's something fierce in his expression. It's like he's a storm about to hit, and the clouds are circling faster and faster.

"I can't do it."

"Wes . . ." I whisper.

"I just can't."

I'm the only one who doesn't jump when the front door slams behind him.

CHAPTER 16

The beat inside the club is so strong that I feel it throbbing in my throat. I lean back against the wall and stare out at the dance floor. In the darkened room I cannot tell where one person ends and another begins; they move together like an angry mob.

The deejay booth is set up in a corner, and I see LJ leaning over a pretty, dark-haired girl. Maria. The Project hasn't found her yet.

Nikki approaches, wobbling slightly on her heels. The Christmas lights hanging from the ceiling turn her face first red, then purple. "You don't drink much, do you?" She yells over the music.

"Why do you say that?"

"Because we've been here over an hour and you haven't even taken a sip."

I shrug, swirling the cheap vodka around in the clear plastic cup. She's wrong: I did take a sip. It tasted like kerosene. "I guess I'm not really in a drinking mood."

One of the dancers bumps into her, and she stumbles forward. I put my hand out to help her, but she waves me away. We are in the depths of an old, abandoned church, and the smell of sweat and perfume can't quite hide the musky odor of long-ago worship. "Did Tag tell you my parents were murdered?" she asks suddenly.

I look over at her, surprised. "I heard him telling Wes."

"It's the anniversary. Four years ago today."

"I'm sorry." I don't know what else to say.

"Sometimes . . . sometimes I wish they had killed me that day."

I shift until I'm facing her. "Don't say that."

She tips back the drink she has in her hand, chugging until it's gone. "God," she gasps. "Why the hell am I telling you this stuff? I must be really drunk."

I want to reach out to her, but I'm not sure how she'll take it. "If you had died, who would look out for LJ?"

She stares down at the dingy floor near our feet. "When I came home and found them, and there was all that blood, I thought that my life had hit rock bottom. That having my parents murdered was as low as it could possibly get. And then we lost the house and had to go on the streets. And then Chris disappeared. That was when I realized that there is no such thing as rock bottom. Life can always get worse, no matter what." Her mouth falls open a little, as though she's shocked she just said so much.

"I hope that's not true."

"That's why I like you, Lydia." Her words come out slightly slurred and I realize she *is* drunk. Very drunk. "You're all sunny and happy." She flings her hand toward my head and drops of vodka from her empty cup fly out and hit me on the cheek. "Not like us. Not hard like me."

"You're not hard."

Nikki laughs, but it's a damaged sound. "Yeah, I am. I've been hard since I walked into the living room and saw pieces of my parents splattered on the walls."

I wince at her words, but she just tries to take another sip from her cup, even though it's empty. "If I didn't have Tag and LJ, I don't know what I would do." Her voice is quieter. "People like me need people like you. That's why you can't give up on Wes."

"I wasn't planning on it."

She drops her cup. "I mean it, Lydia." She leans into me, and I pull back against the wall as the smell of liquor surrounds us both. "He needs you. You're soft where he's hard."

I bristle at her words. "I'm not soft. Just because I didn't grow up on the streets doesn't mean I'm not strong enough to handle myself."

Nikki shakes her head in a scattered movement. "I'm not saying you're weak. But you're innocent. I envy that.

It's why I acted like such a bitch at first." She smirks. "Be glad you're not like the rest of us. You haven't had to shut yourself off in order to survive."

"I don't think I'm innocent." For some reason I feel like I'm going to cry, and I turn away, staring at the pulsing bodies on the dance floor. "Maybe I used to be. But I can feel myself getting harder every day."

"It's not a bad thing to be tough, Lydia. And you are tough, even if it's a different kind of toughness from what I have. But it's not the same as being *hard*. There's a difference." Her words are slurred, but I'm surprised at how articulate she's being. And also curious about why she's chosen me to confide in.

"That's what Wes sees in you." She laughs again. "You pried into my shit—now I'm prying into yours."

"But Wes isn't like that," I respond. "He's not as damaged as you think."

She gives me a strange look, and her body melts into the wall next to me, like she no longer has the energy to hold herself up anymore. "Wes is cold, Lydia. And kind of scary. You're the only person who sees anything else in him. That's what I mean, when I say you're soft. But it doesn't make you weak. It makes you able to see stuff the rest of us can't anymore."

"Tag still sees that in him too." I feel like she's just insulted Wes somehow, and the need to defend him rises up inside of me. "He can look past the front that Wes puts up."

"Tag used to know him and love him. And besides, Tag's a lot like you. Able to find the good in people." Nikki hunches her shoulders like she's trying to hide behind them. "Wes and I are the broken ones. You and Tag are the ones who keep trying to save us from ourselves."

"Wes saves me too. All the time."

"Because he loves you. Isn't that what love is? Saving each other from the shit that life keeps throwing at us?"

I smile a little. "How poetic."

"Just . . . give him a chance. If he's anything like me, he'll keep testing you and trying to push you away and shit. But he loves you, I can tell. And I don't think he's someone who gives that away easily."

I cock my head at her, wondering if she's advocating for Wes or herself. Maybe she thinks that if I can love someone like Wes, then there's hope for someone like her. She pulls away from the wall, and I watch the bright lights play across her dark hair. "No matter what you do, don't let him push you away," she repeats.

I open my mouth, but then Tag is there. He slides an arm around Nikki's waist. "You're drunk, babe," he says.

"No, I need more vodka." Her eyes are glassy and she's having a hard time holding herself up.

"I think it's time to get you home." Tag pulls her toward the entrance. "We'll see you guys back at the squat," he yells to me.

I nod.

Nikki turns around and points one red-tipped finger at me. "Remember what I said, Lydia. It can always get worse, but that doesn't mean you give up."

The music has changed from techno to old-school rap: a guy talking in slow tones over a catchy melody. I glance toward the deejay booth, and then push myself up off of the wall. LJ and Maria have disappeared.

I frantically look around the club. But I can't see anything: it's too dark in here, with too many people. I knew we should have taken Maria and gotten out of here, but LJ didn't want to worry her. He said he would watch out for her during her set, and I agreed, confident that the Montauk Project wouldn't try anything around this many people. But maybe I was wrong.

I head for the nearest exit, but a boy with a shaved head steps in front of me. His lip ring catches the light even in this dim basement. "You're too fine to be sitting in the corner all night," he says. "Let's dance."

"I can't, I'm in a hurry." I try to move past him, but he blocks my path again. "Move," I say.

"Don't be like that."

"I said move." I shove at his chest and he takes a step back. But he grabs my arm before I can get away.

"And I said don't be like that," he snarls, and squeezes my skin hard enough to leave a bruise.

Suddenly he's ripped away from me and knocks into a crowd of people. I hear a shout as someone spills their drink.

Wes is standing in front of me, glaring at the punk kid.

His hair is messier than usual, as though he's been running his fingers through it.

"Wes." I ignore the commotion and focus on him. "We have to find LJ and Maria. They disappeared."

He nods, and we push through the crowd. We find the exit and run up the dusty stone steps. Kids are sitting on them, some drinking and talking, some making out, and we weave around them. Outside, the air is humid, but at least it's not as oppressive as it is in the club. We're on a side street, and there are people everywhere, waiting to get inside or smoking cigarettes.

"I don't see them." I sound panicked.

"There." Wes points to an alley next to the church. We run over to it. A white van is parked on the far end. As I watch, a flash of dark hair disappears into it, and I hear the jagged sound of the door sliding shut.

The van pulls away with a squeal of tires.

"Maria!" I scream and run down the alley. By the time I get to the end, the van is nowhere in sight.

"We have to do something," I pant at Wes. "We have to go after them."

Wes puts his hand on my back. "She's gone, Lydia. They have her now."

"But—"

"We need to find LJ," he says.

"LJ," I repeat, and turn and run back to the club. I hear Wes follow me.

LJ is not outside. He's not on the steps. He's not near the

long line for the bathroom.

"Please let him be okay," I murmur under my breath as we push our way through the dance floor.

I feel someone touch my shoulder. "Lydia."

It's LJ. I throw my arms around him. "You're okay, you're okay," I chant into his ear.

He pulls away from me. "Have you seen Maria? I can't find her anywhere. She said she had to go to the bathroom. I was waiting outside the door, but she never came out. I even went in there. It was empty." He spins around in a circle, wildly searching. We're blocked on all sides by people moving to the rhythm of the music. "We have to find her."

"Let's go somewhere we can talk," Wes says.

LJ's eyes look huge under the tiny lights. "She's gone, isn't she? Oh god, they got her." He buries his face in his hands. "I thought I could save her. I thought I could keep her safe."

He suddenly grabs both my shoulders and shakes me so hard my teeth rattle. "We're next. They'll get us. They'll kill us. We can't run."

I pry his fingers off me. "LJ, we *can*. Maria didn't know they were coming. But we have a chance."

He shakes his head. I reach for him, but he puts his hand out. "No. No. I need to be alone. I need to think about this. I'll . . . I'll see you guys later."

"Wait—"

He disappears into the sea of dancers. I start after him,

but Wes stops me. "Let him go."

"It might not be safe."

"They're not coming for him now. Let him be alone."

It goes against all of my instincts, but I turn away from LJ's departing back.

Wes and I stand in the middle of the dance floor. Even surrounded by people, I feel completely alone. The adrenaline from searching for Maria is wearing off, and the constant beat of the music pounds inside my head.

Wes turns to face me. He bends down until his mouth is next to my ear. "I'm sorry about earlier." I feel his breath against my neck. "The thought of you having anything to do with the Montauk Project makes me crazy. But I shouldn't have acted like that. I won't leave you alone in this."

I lean into him. So he can hear me over the music, I tell myself. "I don't want to be right, if it makes you feel better."

"I hope you're not."

"Me too."

Someone jostles me from behind and I fall forward into his chest. His arms close around me. I want to press against him, to crawl inside of his skin just so I'll know what it feels like to be safe again.

I hook my arms around his neck and slide closer. He freezes for a second, and then he pulls my body against his. I feel his hand clench on my waist, holding me close to him. My face is tucked against his chest. I feel his body move under the dark material of his shirt.

I tilt my head back and our eyes meet. And then his mouth comes down hard on mine, so quickly that I jump a little before sinking into it. This is not a slow kiss. This is hands twisting in hair, tongues molding together, lips and teeth and gasping for air. He grabs my hips tight and pulls my body up against his.

He rips his mouth away and kisses my chin, my collarbone. "I won't let them take you," he repeats over and over against my skin.

"I know. I know."

Someone shouts, loud enough to hear over the music. A murmur spreads through the crowd. Wes lifts his head up.

"Cops!" I hear a girl next to me scream.

People start running for the exit in a stampede. I am thrown against Wes. He curls his hand around my elbow.

I can't see anything except for random bodies moving in every direction, but the crowd is getting louder. Wes and I move in the opposite direction, toward the back of the room. There is a hallway connected to the back wall; a few planks of wood are nailed across what used to be the doorway. I can't see what's beyond it; everything is in shadow.

Without a word of warning, Wes lifts me up and over the wood. I land on my feet with a gasp and turn to see him vault over. He takes my hand again and we run down a long, dark hallway.

We climb a staircase and reach a locked door. Wes

shoves his shoulder into the rotted wood until it breaks free. I hear shouting and loud banging noises that travel up from the basement, though it doesn't sound like anyone followed us.

The door is connected to the main part of the old church, and Wes and I enter a huge room with cathedral ceilings and broken stained-glass windows. We are standing by the altar, near where the priest used to deliver his sermons. I walk slowly down the steps until I reach the aisle. Only a few pews are left on either side; most of the room is empty, covered in debris. There are piles of dirty tarps along one wall, discarded by workmen who abandoned this place years ago.

"We should stay here for a while," Wes says. His voice sounds louder than normal as it bounces off the high ceilings. "There are probably cops outside, arresting whoever comes out of the building."

"Okay." I press my fingers to my lips, thinking of that kiss. It it felt different from any other kiss I've had with Wes. Like it was with someone else entirely.

I glance over at him, and the events of the last few days start flitting through my head: Wes telling me we can't be together, shaking in the bathroom, his too-bright smile at the fountain.

Something is off about him, and it has been since that first night he stole into my bedroom. I've been letting him tell me he's fine, afraid that he'll push me away if I pry too hard. But I can't keep pretending that everything is okay when it's clearly not.

"We need to talk," I say softly.

He walks down the steps too, until he's standing near the pew opposite me, but he doesn't say anything.

"Wes?"

"I . . . there's nothing to talk about."

"There is. I think you're hiding something from me and I think you have been for a long time."

"There's nothing—"

"Stop." My voice is firm. "You're acting so different lately. Erratic. It's like you have no control over what you're feeling. And that shaking . . . I'm worried about you."

"You shouldn't be."

"Fine, then I'm angry with you." And I am, I realize. Wes is the only person left I can count on, but I don't even know how he feels about me. When he brought me to 1989, I thought we would be together. But every move he's made since then has been unpredictable.

"You can't keep pushing me away and then pulling me closer," I say to him. "You're jerking me around and it has to stop."

He clenches his hands together, maybe in an effort not to reach for me, maybe because he's starting to get angry too. "I'm not jerking you around."

"What do you call that back there? Last night you said we can't ever be together. Earlier today you spun me into a fountain, and now you kiss me on some dance floor." I step closer to him. "Did that kiss change anything? Do you want to be with me?"

He doesn't answer.

I whirl around until my back is to him and cross my hands over my chest. I am facing one of the few stained-glass windows that hasn't been cracked or smashed, and I stare at the Virgin Mary on her knees with her hands folded. "It's more than just that, Wes. Something is wrong, and I think it's bigger than you and me. There's something you're not telling me."

"It's complicated."

I turn to face him again. "Then make me understand."

He moves toward me, and I flinch at the fierce look in his eyes. "Why do you have to push so much all the time? Why can't you leave anything alone? You wouldn't even be in this mess if you hadn't inserted yourself into the Project, yet again."

"It doesn't even matter!" I shout the words, and then hear them repeated back as they echo through the empty space. "They're going to find me in the end. I was always destined to become a recruit. Why can't we enjoy the last few days or weeks we have together?"

"Is that what you really want?" Now he's practically shouting too. "A few minutes of happiness before you're condemned to a lifetime of slavery? Of silence?"

"No. It's not what I want." I drop my voice. "What I want is to be with you. I want to fight against our fate. To try and figure out some way to save both of us from the

Project without losing everyone else I love too."

He sighs and stares down at his feet. "I want that too. But it's not possible."

"Why not?"

"It just isn't. They'll always find us. We can't get away from them."

"So that's it?" I throw myself down onto one of the pews. It squeaks under my weight and a puff of dust flies up around me. "They just get to win? To wreck both of our lives?"

"We don't know that's what the list means. They probably don't know about you at all."

"Oh, wake up, Wes. We just watched Maria disappear tonight. I don't know how my name ended up on that list, but I've had this scar my whole life, even before I went back in time. It means something."

He shakes his head. "No. You'll still be safe. You have to live a normal life."

"What's normal?" I stand up again, my hands in fists at my sides. "Was it normal that I ended up going back in time? That my great-grandfather created the program that's responsible for snatching you off the street? That you randomly saw me in the woods one night and that stopped you from killing me when you found me inside the Facility? We're so far beyond normal, Wes. I don't think my life can ever go back to that."

He steps forward and closes his hands over my shoulders. "It has to."

"Why? What are you so afraid of? Why can't we work together to figure out a solution to this?"

"There is no solution. I'm condemned to this life, but you can still get away."

But I'm on a roll now, and I barely hear him. "Why were you shaking the other day in the bathroom? What are you hiding from me?"

"Nothing."

"The mood swings. The twitching. The pushing and the pulling. You can't think I wouldn't notice that something is wrong."

"I . . ."

"Don't shut me out anymore," I whisper.

"I'm not trying to. I just . . . don't know how to deal with this." His grip is almost painfully tight.

I go still. "Deal with what, Wes?"

"I'm . . ." He clenches his jaw and turns away.

"Wes." I move in close to him. "I came to the past for you. There's nothing you can tell me that will change how I feel. I'll do anything to help you. You have to trust me."

"I don't think even you can help me this time, Lydia." His voice cracks.

"Try me."

He closes his eyes. "I'm dying, Lydia. And I don't know how to stop it from happening."

CHAPTER 17

We sit side by side on the dirty pew. Wes is so motionless that I'm not sure he's even breathing anymore.

I keep his hand clasped in mine and wait until he's ready to speak.

It takes a few minutes for him to start. "Seventeen killed herself, but it wasn't because the Project was investigating her."

I think back to that broken look on his face, the night he came to my room. I had never seen him so upset. Until now, maybe.

"Her body was starting to show signs of deteriorating," he explains. "I saw it that night on patrol. She was shaking, her concentration was off. She couldn't hear as well, couldn't see things that were right in front of her. As soon as

I saw her, I knew she didn't have long before they realized she was done." He pauses and gives me a sideways glance. "She was already nineteen. Had been traveling through time for the past eight years. The TM was wearing her body down. It happens to all of the recruits, eventually. Once the Project notices, they dispose of us."

I force myself to ask, "How? What do they do exactly?"

His fingers spasm in mine, and I bear down hard on our joined hands until it stops. "They kill us, but not right away. First the scientists use our bodies for research, to study how much damage the TM does. It's rare that a recruit even makes it to eighteen or nineteen; most of us die in the field before then. It's why the older recruits are more valuable. They're usually . . ." His voice falters a little and I press into his shoulder. "Alive. For the experiments. At least in the beginning."

"God."

"Sometimes it even happens when we're conscious." He sounds remote, detached. Pretending he's not afraid. "Getting samples from a live person is the best way to get results."

"So Seventeen killed herself," I say softly. "To not go through that."

He nods. "But as soon as I saw her that night, I knew I wasn't far behind. I was starting to twitch sometimes. Small stuff, but it had never happened before that. And I'm eighteen now, in my time." His mouth twists. "Happy birthday to me."

"Wes . . ."

"It's why I had to see you that night when I came to your room. I didn't know how much time I had left. And then you begged me to take you with me, and I couldn't say no. I just wanted to be near you before it was too late. But then we kissed in the subway, and I knew it wasn't fair to you. It was selfish to put you at risk. To pretend that we could have a future together when we can't." He sighs. "I know I've been acting strange, but I just don't know how to deal with this. Maybe if you hadn't come into my life, it might have been different. I might have stayed cold, I might have even welcomed it. But now . . ."

"I would have understood if you had told me."

He gives me a half smile. "No, you wouldn't have. You would have done everything in your power to try and save me."

I open my mouth to argue, but he cuts me off. "That's the type of person you are, Lydia. Always trying to save the people you care about. You never give up, even when it seems hopeless. You make me believe in the impossible. It's why I fell in love with you in the first place."

My body feels like ice, but at his words, the coldness thaws a little inside of me. "You've never said that before." I pronounce each word carefully.

He shifts on the bench until he's facing me. The curve of his mouth is drawn and serious. "I love you, Lydia, as much as someone like me is capable of loving anyone."

"I love you too." I reach up and cup his face in my

hands. "Which is how I know that you're capable of loving just like anyone else. I believe that with my whole self," I say fiercely. "And we *will* find a way to save you from this. It's not impossible."

"Lydia." He grabs my wrists and pulls my hands away. "I don't know how much time I have left. It's . . . getting worse, since we came back here. I might only have one or two more jumps through time in me."

"Then we'll go to the nineteen twenties or something." I try to keep my voice light, but it comes out shaky and unsure. "I've always wanted to be a flapper."

He gives me that half smile again, only this time it just looks sad. "I'm not doing that to you. I'm not taking you away from your family."

"What family?" I ignore the ache that is trying to tear its way through my chest. "My grandpa is crazy, my parents are like strangers. I don't have much of a life left in two thousand twelve."

The pew under us squeaks as he quickly stands up. "No. We'll save your grandfather and fix the future. Then your life will be normal again, and you can go back home."

I shake my head. "You're ignoring that list again. If I go back home, they might come for me even if we do manage to change the future. Our only hope is to evade them. Or maybe that rebellion is real, and the Resister will pop up at any moment and take us away from here."

He makes a frustrated sound and slides his hand over his chin.

"There's no way to win, is there?" My voice is small.

"I meant what I said, Lydia." He reaches for my arm and pulls me off the bench until I'm standing close to him. "I won't let them take you."

"I want to believe you Wes, but I don't know how either of us can fix this." I lean forward and rest my head against his chest. "In every scenario, I lose someone I love."

I feel his hand come up and gently cup the back of my neck.

We are both silent. There's nothing left to say.

By the time we get back, the squat is dark and quiet. There's a low buzzing light on in LJ's room, but, for once, I can't hear the clattering of computer keys. "I think everyone's asleep already."

Wes slides his shoes off. "It's late."

I fall onto the lumpy couch. "I want to sleep for a million years."

Wes smiles.

I watch as he settles on the floor next to me. His sports jacket is already lying there from last night, and he begins to fold it into a makeshift pillow. "Wes." We haven't turned on any lights, but the room is dimly lit by the streetlamp outside. "Will you . . ." He stops what he's doing and gives me a curious look. "I was thinking . . ." I trace a pattern in the ratty material of the couch and blurt it out. "Will you stay with me?"

"I'm right here, Lydia."

"No, I mean, will you sleep . . . here? With me?"

His face goes blank. "You want me to sleep on the couch with you?"

I nod, though I still can't meet his eyes. "I want to know that we're both safe. At least for tonight."

He opens his mouth, then shuts it slowly. "Okay."

I sit up as he stands and moves the short distance to the couch. He sits down next to me. There's an awkward pause as we both hesitate, neither of us quite sure what to do. Finally, Wes slides his arm around my waist and lies down on his side, pulling me along with him. His other hand wraps around my stomach. I am resting in the cradle of his arms, and his face is pressed against the top of my head. I can feel every breath he takes.

We're both still, aware of each other's bodies in a way we never have been before. I close my eyes at the feeling of being completely surrounded by him. The tension slowly drains out of me, and I sink further into the couch and into Wes. Behind me, Wes relaxes too, and his breathing becomes low and steady.

But even this is not enough to erase the memory of what I learned tonight, and after a minute I whisper into the dark, "If we don't find a way for you to escape, what will happen to you? Would you let them kill you?"

"No." He doesn't finish, but he doesn't have to; I know exactly what he'll do—he'll make the same choice Seventeen did.

I wind my fingers through the hand that's wrapped

around my stomach. I walked away from Wes once and it almost killed me. But even then I had hope that he was alive and somewhere in the world. I can't leave him again, knowing that he's going to die soon.

In that moment, I make a choice.

"We're going to nineteen twenty." My voice is quiet but resolved.

"We've been over this, Lydia."

"No." I stay facing away from him and watch the shadows play across the bruised and battered wooden floor. I hear a garbage truck rumble past the window, and a high beeping noise as it backs up near the curb. "It's not about you sacrificing yourself anymore, Wes. We're both in danger now. We'll save my grandfather, make the future right again, and then figure out a way to use the TM to get away from all of this."

"What about your life?" His voice is even softer than a whisper, and if his mouth wasn't pressed against my hair, I wouldn't be able to hear him. "What about your family?"

"We'll be each other's family."

His arms tighten around me.

I wait, but he doesn't say anything else. His breathing changes, deepens, and I shut my eyes. I am almost asleep when I hear him say, softly, "Okay. We'll go."

I smile into the dark.

CHAPTER 18

Wake up."

I crack my eyes open. I am lying on the couch alone; Wes is no longer tucked in behind me.

But Nikki is there, standing over me and holding out an orange.

"What do you want?" I groan, turning away from her.

She pokes me in the shoulder. "I brought you food. You could at least be grateful."

I slowly rise to a sitting position, and I rub at the hair that has plastered itself to the side of my face.

"I'm grateful. Though I'd probably be a lot more grateful if you let me sleep."

She shrugs and tosses the orange at me. I don't even attempt to catch it and it lands heavily in my lap. "No one's here, and Tag just left to go tag some trains uptown. I'm bored."

I raise an eyebrow. "Tag went to tag?"

"You know, graffiti. He's always been into tagging. It's how he got the nickname in the first place." She gives me a "duh" look.

I grab the orange and stand up. "Where's Wes?"

"I have no idea. He's been gone all morning."

I frown, wondering where he could have gone. Maybe to follow McGregor, though there doesn't seem to be much point to it now. We've basically solved the mystery of why he lost the election. "What time is it?"

"Ten."

"Aren't you hungover?" I ask her.

"Like you wouldn't believe."

I toss the orange back at Nikki and reach for my blue dress. It's starting to smell a little. I pull it on anyway.

"What are you doing today?" Nikki sits down at the table and bites into a green apple.

"I don't know." Wes and I didn't talk specifics about our plan, but I can't leave with him until I know that my grandfather is safe. And I also need to find out where that disk came from. Could the Resister have given it to Grandpa? Does it have something to do with this mysterious rebellion?

It's time to tell my grandfather the truth about who I am. He may have freaked out before, but if anyone's going to believe I'm a time traveler, it's him. And maybe once he knows I'm his granddaughter, he'll trust me enough to give me some answers.

Which means that as soon as Wes gets back, we need to go back to Bellevue.

"Actually, I do have plans," I say to Nikki. "Wes and I have something we need to do. I guess I'm waiting for him."

Nikki smiles. "We could hang, if you want. I have cards."

I smile back, wondering if she remembers telling me about her parents, and making me promise to never give up on Wes. "Sure." She stands up to get them, but I stop her. "Have you seen LJ today?"

She nods. "He left a few hours ago, said he needed to walk around or something. He was really quiet."

"Isn't he always quiet?"

"Not like this. I saw Maria with him last night; she probably rejected him or something. He's been chasing her for years."

Her words make my stomach twist. Poor LJ.

I watch Nikki get up from the table, and her curly brown hair bounces around her shoulders. There is something lighter about her, softer, and I wonder if telling me that stuff last night took a weight off her. Sometimes you just need to talk, even if it is to a relative stranger.

Poor Nikki.

The only way for LJ to make it through this is to go into hiding, which probably means leaving Nikki behind. She'll lose another brother, and she'll never know the reason why.

I guess she was right—it can always get worse. I just pray this won't be the thing that makes her finally give up.

I hang out with Nikki for an hour. Then two. Then four. Wes still doesn't come back, but LJ does. He gives us both a dark look before disappearing into his bedroom. Nikki just rolls her eyes.

I want to help him, but I'm starting to worry about Wes. Why would he be tailing McGregor for this long? It doesn't make sense. I watch the sun fall toward the horizon. If I don't leave soon, I won't be able to see my grandfather before visiting hours end.

"I'm booored," Nikki says from the couch. "Let's go out."

"I can't. There's something I need to do." I walk to the door. "I'll be back later. If Wes comes by, tell him . . . that I went uptown. To see my uncle. He'll know where I am."

"Where are you going?" She narrows her eyes.

"Just tell him." I am about to leave the squat, but something makes me detour into LJ's room. He is sitting at his computer. Not typing, just staring at it.

"I'm going out for a bit," I say softly. "But I want to make sure you're going to be okay."

He looks up at me. "How do I survive this?" he whispers.

"I don't know," I tell him honestly. "But you have to try. You know when they're coming. They won't expect you to have that information. You already have a head start."

"So I just run for the rest of my life?"

"Maybe. But you can also fight, LJ. Find out who this Resister is, and what he means by the rebellion. Fight against your fate."

He twists in his chair until he's facing me. "Is that what you're doing?"

I smile a little. "I'm trying to. I'll let you know how it goes."

"I don't want to lose everything." His voice is quiet. "Nikki . . . it will crush her."

I think of Mary, laughing as she splashed in the ocean in Montauk. Of Hannah, making a face at me over a plate of fries. Of Saturday mornings around the breakfast table with my mom and dad and grandpa. "If they love you, I don't think you can ever really lose them," I say thickly. "Even if you're not in the same place."

"I hope that's true." He turns around again. "I'll see you soon, Lydia."

I stare at his thin shoulders. Even though he's almost fourteen, he looks too small for the burdens I heaped on top of him. "Yeah, soon."

I pause at the door. "Don't let them win, LJ."

He doesn't answer, and I leave the room.

I make it to Bellevue just in time. A woman at the front desk directs me to the psych ward again, since I can't remember how to find it myself. As soon as I'm outside the heavy, fortified door, I lay on the buzzer, waiting for a nurse to let me in.

It takes a few minutes before the door opens a crack. A face peers out at me. It's the same bald male nurse from two days ago. "Hi," I say a little breathlessly. "Do you remember me?"

He looks confused for a moment, but then nods and smiles. "Bentley's niece. You made it in the nick of time, didn't you?"

"It's still visiting hours, isn't it?"

"Yes, but that's not what I mean. Didn't you hear? Your uncle is getting moved today."

A flicker of alarm shoots through me. As far as I know, Grandpa never left Bellevue in this version of the time line. "Getting moved to where?"

"The long-term patient care facility at Rockland Hospital. I told you about it last time, remember?"

"Yes," I respond slowly. "But I didn't think it was happening so soon."

The nurse shrugs. "The people from Rockland showed up today. Said they're ready for him now. It was a little out of the blue, but these things happen." He gestures over his shoulder. "They're in with him, if you want to go say goodbye."

The flicker grows into a sharp, nervous pang. "I want to see him."

The nurse lets me into the ward and leads me down

the hall again, but halfway there another nurse stops him. They murmur for a while, and then the bald nurse turns to me. "I'm sorry, I need to go take care of something. You remember where his room is, right? The Rockland transport team is highly trained, so there shouldn't be a repeat of last time."

"I'll be fine."

He smiles and walks back down the hall.

I slowly approach my grandfather's room. There's a rustling sound from the partially open doorway, and I hear a female voice bark out an order.

I creep closer and peek through the crack in the door. There are three people in the room. One is older, male, and dressed as a doctor. The other two are wearing orderly uniforms. I realize that one of them is a girl around my age. She has pretty, delicate features and light brown skin. "Move him," she orders the two men. "We're running out of time. Doctor Peters is expecting us soon."

The doctor and the other male orderly walk to the head of the bed and lift up the prone figure of my grandfather. As they dump him onto a waiting gurney, I see that he's unconscious, or drugged maybe, and wrapped in a thin white sheet.

"Careful," the girl snaps. "He's not supposed to be harmed."

The nurse didn't mention that my grandfather was going to be drugged for the transport. And why are two older men, including a doctor, taking orders from this young girl? There's something about her voice . . . something robotic and flat that reminds me of how Wes spoke in the beginning. No inflection. No emotion.

The girl moves to one of the freestanding closets in the room. She stands on her tiptoes in order to reach a blanket on the top shelf. When she does, the short sleeve of her pale blue uniform rides up her arm. I gasp out loud. There, against her skin, is a white, raised bump. *The Mark of the Traveler.* No wonder the other men were taking orders from her; she's a recruit for the Montauk Project, and they must be guards sent to help her kidnap my grandfather.

Grandpa wasn't supposed to disappear for another three days, but clearly the time line has changed again. Only this time the Montauk Project must be aware of it. Why else would they be kidnapping him? Have I done something else to alter history?

The girl suddenly turns her head toward the hallway and our eyes meet. I half expect her to smile and start pretending she's a representative from Rockland; I know from experience that the recruits are supposed to maintain cover at all times. But her eyes narrow and she begins walking quickly toward the door—toward me. "Watch the main target," she says over her shoulder to the men, not even bothering to put any inflection in her voice. "I have to take care of this."

I don't like the look in her eyes. She knows me somehow,

and her gaze has turned predatory and fierce. I whip around and sprint down the hallway.

I run straight into the bald nurse and grasp the front of his shirt in both hands. "Give me your key," I pant.

"What?"

"Your key! I need to get out of here."

"I don't—"

I don't have time for this; the girl is headed right for us. She can't run without drawing too much attention to herself, but I can still feel her quickly approaching. I grab the key that hangs around the nurse's neck and yank as hard as I can. The thin clasp that connects it to a braided cord snaps neatly in half. The nurse sputters behind me as I run for the exit.

My hand slips on the metal and I almost drop the key twice. From farther down the hallway, I hear the recruit and the male nurse exchange words, and then the sound of rapid footsteps coming closer.

Concentrate, Lydia.

I manage to fit the key into the lock and pry the door open. The corridor in front of me is empty; the rest of this hospital floor seems practically deserted. I run blindly down the beige-colored hallway, looking for a way out. In the background, I hear the door to the psych ward slam open and the sound of someone's feet swiftly pounding on the floor. The recruit is chasing me down.

There's a red exit sign up ahead; it's hanging above a

door that connects to the stairs. I throw it open and take the steps two, three at a time. The stairwell is empty and sterile, lit with an artificial, grayish light. I make it down one flight before I hear her on the stairs above me. Now that she's out of the ward she is gaining speed. I push forward, even though my lungs and legs are starting to burn.

I whip around a corner, but I'm not quick enough. She barrels into my side and we both crash into the far wall. My head bounces on the concrete.

It hurts, but the fear is worse than the physical pain. I've seen Wes fight; I have no shot against someone like him.

The girl grabs my arm and yanks me forward. I twist away and try to hit her with my left hand. She blocks it easily and locks her arm around mine. She angles my body in front of hers, holding me with one arm while she reaches into her pocket for something.

We're about the same height, but she's smaller, thin and wiry, and I use the difference in our size to my advantage. Throwing my body forward, I knock her off balance. Whatever was in her hand crashes down to the ground as she tries to keep her grip on me.

"Why are you doing this?" I speak through clenched teeth as we struggle against each other.

"Quiet." She squeezes harder, and I gasp as the breath leaves my body. This girl may be small, but she has the strength of a bear. I twist and turn and somehow manage to get one of my arms free. But even though I scratch and pry at the hand she has locked around my waist, she doesn't let go. Remembering that I have more than two limbs, I lift my right leg and kick backward into her knee. She wobbles slightly but doesn't go down.

What is it you're supposed to do when a bear attacks? Play dead?

I go limp in her arms. She makes a small, surprised noise right before we both tumble onto the ground.

She never breaks her grasp, but I manage to roll onto my hands and knees with her attached to me like some kind of oversized barnacle. I try to crawl forward, but she knocks my legs out from under me and I fall onto my side. One of her hands leaves my waist and I see her reaching for a syringe that's lying on the floor near our heads. It must have been what she dropped earlier; she's going to drug me like she did my grandfather.

One of my arms is still free and I drive it behind me, elbowing her hard in the gut. The arm around me loosens. I scramble away, but she launches herself onto my back again. This time her entire weight is pinning me down, and she secures my arms and legs in a wrestler-style hold. I can't move a muscle.

I hear her reach for the syringe again, and I struggle even harder, but it's useless. I open my mouth to scream and realize in horror I can't even do that; I have no breath for it, not with the girl perched on top of my lungs.

My head is turned to the side, and I see that we're right

next to the edge of the stairs. Then I feel the needle prick into my arm. Terror floods through me and I use all of my strength to heave onto my side, tilting my body in an effort to buck her off.

The movement shifts the girl off balance. She doesn't have time to stop herself before she tumbles headfirst down the stairwell, hitting each step with a sickening thud.

I stagger to my feet. The syringe has sunk all the way into my skin, but I don't think she had time to release any of the contents. I pull it out with a wince and throw it onto the ground. The girl is immobile at the bottom of the stair-case. I grab the banister and ease my way down the stairs until I'm standing over her body. I can't tell if she's dead, so I kneel and put my fingers on her neck. She has a pulse, thank god. I wouldn't want to be responsible for killing someone, even if she was trying to drug me. In the end we're all just victims of the Montauk Project.

But that doesn't mean I'm going to stick around wait-ing for her to wake up. I stand up again, using the banister to steady myself. My feet feel thick and heavy, but there's a weightlessness to my head that's unsettling. Did I hit it harder than I thought? I try to take a step down the stairs, but I only slide along the side of the wall. My knees give out, and I sink onto the floor.

I have one moment of clarity, one moment of panic as I realize that I must have been injected with some of that drug. But then my thoughts dissolve, and the stairwell spins in a hazy circle. I fall over to the side, my head resting on the ground next to the recruit. If her eyes were open, we would be staring at each other.

I close mine too. The black behind my eyelids is endless.

CHAPTER 19

I come to slowly and blink in the artificial light. I am lying on my side on a hard bed, facing a dull gray wall. I carefully stretch. My fingers feel like the bones have welded together, and I hear them pop as I move my hands out in front of my body.

What happened at Bellevue rushes back, and I sit up quickly. I close my eyes and wait for the world to steady. As soon as the nausea subsides, I open my eyes again. I am in a small room with no windows and only one fortified door.

I hear a low moaning noise, and I turn to see my grandfather lying on the white tile floor, tucked in next to the low cot I'm sitting on.

I scramble off the bed, falling to my knees next to his hunched figure.

"Grandpa," I whisper, and lay my hands on his shoulders. When I touch him, he flinches away from me with a shriek. "Grandpa." The word is broken this time, a low, fractured sound.

I don't try to touch him again. Instead I slowly stand up and look around the room. It is clearly a cell, though it doesn't look like the ones they threw Wes and me into in Montauk. We must still be in New York City, in the holding area of the Center.

Did they attack me when they discovered I wasn't Seventeen? That I was somehow responsible for the rift in time? Or were they after my grandfather and the information he had on that disk? Maybe I was just a casualty of his abduction.

But as soon as the recruit saw me, she attacked. It was too personal to be a coincidence. They wanted *me* for some reason. But why? Have they finally decided to bring me in, to force me to become a recruit?

I hear a heaving sound, and a sour, sickly smell fills the air. I turn back to my grandfather. He has thrown up all over himself, and he's rocking back and forth in the vomit. Where is Wes? Does he even know I was taken?

I kneel next to my grandfather again. But every time I touch him, he recoils. Finally I just sit next to him and hum a tuneless song under my breath. It seems to calm him.

I fight tears as I stare at the heavy metal door that separates me from freedom. I'm not sure how long I sit there with my grandfather, reliving the past few days, wondering where I went wrong, but I'm jolted back to the present by a scraping noise at the door. I freeze as it opens slowly.

It's Wes, wearing his black recruit uniform. He slips quietly into the room.

"Oh my god," I breathe. I stumble to my feet, almost tripping in my effort to reach him. "You're here."

My arms close around his. He is stiff, though he relaxes for a second, his hands coming up to lightly touch my back. But then he steps away from me.

We have to maintain cover. "What's going on?" I whisper the words, trying not to move my mouth. "Do you know why they took me? How they found out about me?"

He doesn't answer, but his gaze falls on my grandfather.

"We need to get him out," I say. I rush back across the room until I'm standing near the bed and Grandpa. "We can take him with us to nineteen twenty. It's the only way now." I look up at Wes.

He still hasn't moved.

"I can't lift him alone. Help me?"

But Wes is silent.

I cannot place the look on his face—it is a combination of horror, regret, and fear. "What's going on?" This time I don't bother to whisper.

I hear a noise from the hallway. It sounds like thunder or a racetrack when the horses start sprinting toward the finish line. I stare up at Wes and watch as his previous expression is slowly wiped away until there is nothing left. He is a hollow shell.

The door bursts open and guards swarm into the room. I scramble to my feet. One of the guards grabs my shoulder. I fight back, lashing out with my arms and legs. I hit him in the knee and he falls, but there's another one and then another, all coming for me. Together, two of the guards take hold of my arms, twisting them painfully behind my back.

"Wes!" I cry out.

I turn to the door, expecting to see him fighting, a pile of guards already at his feet. But he is just standing there; the soldiers rush past like he's a rock in a stream, calmly parting the water in front of him.

"Wes?" My voice falls away as our eyes meet.

"Take the girl into an empty cell," he says. "General Walker needs to question her."

His face is no longer blank, but I almost wish it were. Because his expression is colder than anything I've ever seen, and it's directed right at me.

That's when I start to suspect I've been betrayed.

CHAPTER 20

This can't be happening. Wes wouldn't work against me. Not him. Anyone but him. I hold his gaze as the guards pull me from the room. He never loses his severe expression, and never softens, not even for a moment.

As I am forced out into the hallway, I glance back over my shoulder. My grandfather is still lying on the floor, slowly rocking. Sick, weak, and oblivious to what has just happened.

"Grandpa!" I scream. But he doesn't look up.

The guards pull me across the hallway and throw me into a new cell. I land on my hands and knees on the hard tile. Wes is nowhere in sight.

The door shuts with a bang. I stay on my knees, my head down, my eyes unfocused as I stare at the blinding white of the floor. Soon I am completely numb.

I crawl forward and see that this room is identical to the one I was in before. I slowly heave myself up onto the bare mattress. How could Wes just stand there, letting the guards take me? It doesn't make sense. Why didn't he give me some kind of sign? Could he have been working with them this whole time, plotting to bring me in?

No. I pull myself up into a sitting position and push my bangs off my forehead with so much force they flutter up over my head. I trust Wes. There has to be a reason for his silence, for why he couldn't help me just now. He would never deliberately hurt me. He'd never hand me over to the Montauk Project, not when he has spent so much time trying to protect me from them.

Any minute now that door will burst open and Wes will be there, and he'll explain everything. I have to be ready to escape with him.

I hear the muffled sound of voices speaking, and the squeak of a boot on the tiled floor outside. *See?* I say to myself. Wes is already here. I stand up and face the door.

The door swings open and I jerk forward automatically, expecting Wes. But it isn't him.

A middle-aged man enters. A younger guard follows him, carrying a metal folding chair, which he places in the center of the room. The young guard then leaves, closing the door firmly behind him.

The older man sits down and gives me a measured look.

His hair is brown, with only touches of gray at his temples, and he's wearing a black uniform, though his is slightly different from the guards'. I see a gold, triangular metal gleaming at his shoulder.

"Lydia Bentley," he says gravely. "We meet at last."

At the sound of his voice, I sink back down onto the white mattress. This is General Walker, the man who debriefed Wes and me when we arrived in 1989. The man who looked at me as if he knew exactly who I was. Now I'm starting to wonder if he did.

"I think we've already met." My voice sounds surprisingly strong. Much stronger than I feel right now.

He leans forward in his chair and rests his elbows on his knees. "But you were pretending to be Seventeen then. So I'm not sure it counts."

When I first saw General Walker, I thought he had a kind face, with crinkly hazel eyes. But I can't find any of that kindness in him now. He just looks calculating and slightly pleased, as though he has won some game I didn't even know we were playing.

"You knew who I was, didn't you?" I ask softly.

"Not then. We did think you were Seventeen, until our recruits in twenty-twelve found her body stashed in the woods yesterday. From there, we were quickly able to ascertain who had taken over her identity." He smiles. "We've known about you for a very long time, Miss Bentley."

I twist my fingers together on my lap. "How?"

"For several reasons." He sits back in his chair, his eyes never leaving my face. "Eleven informed me that you found your name on a list of our recruits. So, you know that we've been tracking you ever since you were born. Or should I say, as soon as you *will* be born."

My breath is short. "Wes wouldn't tell you that."

He smiles. Walker is distinguished-looking, with a long, patrician nose and a high forehead. None of this can quite hide how cruel his eyes are, though. "Are you sure you know *Wes* as well as you think you do?"

"What does that mean?"

But he doesn't answer my question. "Eleven also said that you discovered what the scar on your shoulder means. I have to say, I'm impressed that you put it all together."

I close my hand around my upper arm, and I feel the round bump under my fingers. "It is from the serum, then? You injected me with something when I was a baby, didn't you?"

"Polypenamaether was invented by a Doctor Faust in nineteen forty-five. It's a type of vaccine, and when injected into the bloodstream it better equips people to handle the TM. Of course children are still able to travel more easily than adults. And even with the drug, the TM is so physically demanding that it will break down the body of any traveler, eventually."

Like Wes, who told me he was dying, who wanted to run away with me.

Then the significance of what the general is saying hits me. Doctor Faust invented the serum that allows me to travel through time safely, and I've had it in my system for my entire life.

"Why are you telling me this?" I demand.

"This is information we share with all of our recruits, eventually."

"But I'm not . . ."

"You are now." He says it as though I should be excited. "You're a recruit, Lydia. It is your destiny."

"I'm not." I jump up from the bed. "I refuse."

"Sit down," he growls.

"No. I'm not yours to control and I never will be. I'm not some scared little kid you picked up off the streets."

"We have your grandfather. According to Eleven, you'll do whatever I say to keep him safe."

I slowly sink back down onto the mattress. According to Eleven? How could Wes tell him that?

I glare at the general. "Why me? I'm seventeen. I'm too old already. And I'm not trained."

Walker steeples his fingers together and considers me over the top of them. "Let me tell you why this election was so important for us. In this time line, because John McGregor loses, Alan Sardosky wins the election. In a few more years, he goes on to become mayor. Then, eventually, a U.S. senator. In the year twenty forty-four, at the age of seventy-three, he will run for the presidency and win. He's an older candidate, but by then, people are living a lot longer. In twenty fifty, during his second term, he signs a nuclear arms act. Two months later, war breaks out between North Korea and the United States. Nuclear bombs are sent to Los Angeles, New York City, Chicago, Boston, and Washington, DC. Millions die. Our Center in New York is destroyed and we lose hundreds of recruits. On a larger scale, the world is never quite the same again."

"No," I whisper. I'm clenching my hands together so hard it feels like my skin is about to split open. "That's impossible."

Walker's expression is solemn. "I'm afraid it's not."

Somewhere in the back of my mind, Wes is telling me that recruits never traveled before 1950 or after 2050. Now I guess I know why.

"I can't . . . that doesn't make sense. The time line changed. Just change it back."

"It's not always that simple."

"But there has to be a way," I say.

"That's where you come in."

I glare at him. "Are you saying this is somehow connected to me becoming a recruit?"

"I'm realizing now that it's more complicated than even I knew. You made the link between John McGregor and Peter Bentley. That was a crucial connection that we did not have. As we speak, we have recruits traveling through time, figuring out where the original rift took place, the one that eventually effected McGregor's defeat. It's like a stack of dominoes. Your grandfather may have changed McGregor, but what happened to change your grandfather?" He raises an eyebrow. "I suspect we can attribute it to your unauthorized trip to nineteen forty-four with Eleven."

"You knew we were in nineteen forty-four," I breathe.

He continues as though I never spoke. "After Eleven brought us the information on McGregor, we were able to piece together your connection to the shift in the time line. Something you did in the nineteen forties changed the future. And now, the Montauk Project is in jeopardy. Now, the world is a different place."

I feel my mouth fall open. "You're saying it's my fault there's a nuclear war."

"I'm saying you're connected in some way."

"I don't believe that."

He shrugs. "The origin of the time line shift and your involvement is new information to us. But you were on our radar long before this, Lydia." He leans closer. "In exactly six months, we send a team of recruits into the future to stop the nuclear holocaust. They are able to infiltrate Sardosky's inner circle and discover his motivations behind his decision. They don't stop him, not yet, but they come close. You are part of that team, Lydia."

I slowly shake my head. "It doesn't matter. The world ends anyway."

"So far, yes. But we've been experimenting with possible

futures. Having you on the team is the closest we've come to preventing Sardosky from signing that act."

"This doesn't make sense." I scowl at the general. "Why wouldn't you just kill him when he was a child? Wouldn't that solve all of your problems?"

"The time line is a little trickier than that. Killing Sardosky accomplishes nothing. The ripple effects through the time line are insurmountable."

I swallow. "You say it as though you've already tried that option."

He smiles. "Of course we have. We've also tried rigging the election. We've tried killing Sardosky's parents, before they even met. But none of those things worked, and in some cases the nuclear attacks came sooner rather than later. The closest we've ever come has been through you and a few other carefully selected recruits."

"But now you know where the shift in the time line came from. Can't you just go back and fix it?"

"No." He studies me with narrowed eyes. "*You* know where the shift came from. And now we have you and we can do what we want with you. Perhaps we'll send you to nineteen forty-four first, to see if you can't fix your mistake. Or maybe we'll have you go kill your younger self."

"You wouldn't."

He chuckles lightly. "Probably not. It would create an entirely new time line, and we can't take that chance."

"Is that why you didn't take me when I was younger?"

I ask. "I've always had this scar, even before I traveled to nineteen forty-four. That means you gave me the serum the day I was born. My name must have always been on that list."

"I cannot comment on the other time line, but I can tell you that every capture of a recruit is precisely timed. Even if it is an orphan we find on the streets. We track them. We learn their history. We know who their great-great grandparents are. We often know more about our recruits than they ever know about themselves. Most importantly, we wait for the exact right moment to take them. You were not ready until your seventeenth year. We had been planning to acquire you in your own time, but then you conveniently landed on our doorstep."

"I didn't land on your doorstep," I say bitterly. "You kidnapped me."

He smirks a little, and his heavy, gray-brown eyebrows draw closer together. "Ah yes. Eleven helped with that, you know. He has been tracking you for a very long time."

I remain still.

"Did he tell you what he does for us?"

"He said . . ." I bite my lip. "He said he gathers information and makes small changes in the time line."

"Sometimes. But he's also one of the main recruits in charge of extraction." I must look confused, because he adds, "Bringing in recruits."

"You mean kidnapping." I think of all those times Wes

shut down while he was talking about the Project snatching children off the streets. I assumed he didn't want to relive the memory of when it happened to him, but maybe he didn't want to be reminded of what they forced him to do to others.

General Walker shrugs. "He was assigned to you, Lydia. He's been following you for months. Long before you stumbled into the TM in twenty twelve."

I shake my head. "I don't believe that."

"Once we realized that you had assumed Seventeen's identity and that you were in nineteen eighty-nine, we knew we needed to bring you in before you could do anything else to disrupt the time line. Eleven had a mission planned for yesterday afternoon, but all of our people were on high alert and instructed to bring you in if they saw you. That's why Twenty-nine apprehended you when she was on her mission to secure your grandfather. She thought she could kill two birds with one stone, so to speak."

Was Wes really heading a mission to turn me in—after we had planned to run away together, after we spent the night wrapped in each other's arms? "Wes wouldn't do that to me. He loves me." But even I am starting to hear the doubt in my voice.

The general stands up and walks over to the door. He raps on the metal once and it immediately opens. "Bring in Eleven," he says to the guard standing outside.

"Yes, sir."

I stare at the door. In less than a minute Wes appears, and my breath catches in my throat. He doesn't look at me as he enters the room.

"Wes." I stand up. "Tell me it's not true. This is a mistake. It has to be."

"Eleven, please explain your objective to Lydia," General Walker says, his voice less familiar and more commanding.

Wes stares blankly at the wall. "I was assigned to follow Lydia Bentley and to do whatever was necessary to bring her into the Project on July thirtieth, two thousand twelve at exactly 10:57 P.M. This objective was made more difficult when I had to follow her to nineteen forty-four. I made sure the target returned safely, but she had grown attached to me and I was forced to change my strategy for her detainment. I brought her to nineteen eighty-nine because I knew it would be easier to turn her in here, when she was willingly disconnected from her friends and family."

I close my eyes so I won't have to look at his face.

I hear Wes say, "It became imperative to persuade the subject I had romantic feelings for her in order to convince her to trust me. It was an unavoidable part of the mission."

I make a small, jagged sound in the back of my throat and squeeze both hands tightly against my chest. "I don't believe it. I don't! You're just saying this because he's here."

Walker's chair scrapes on the tile and I open my eyes to see him walking toward the door. "I'll give you two a minute." He sounds amused. "And Lydia? There are no cameras in this room."

Then Wes and I are alone.

I spare two seconds to look at the corners of the ceiling. The general is right; I can't see any cameras. Moving quickly, I launch myself across the room and take Wes's arm. "What is going on? Please tell me you have a plan."

"I don't know what you're talking about." His voice is still cold.

"Wes, he's gone," I say desperately. "We're alone."

He stares into my face and I jerk back at the vacant look in his eyes. This is not the Wes I know. I've never seen this person before.

"It doesn't change anything. Finding you was a mission. Now you have been delivered to the Project and the mission has been completed."

It's not until I taste the salt that I realize I'm crying. The tears drip down my face. One falls onto Wes's foot, a tiny drop that disappears into the blackness of his boot. "Why didn't you turn me in when we got back from nineteen forty-four? Or when we first came to eighty-nine? Why did you wait so long?"

"Those events weren't close enough to the time I was instructed to bring you in. Now it is. The timing of our missions is precise."

I shake my head back and forth and dig my fingers into the stretchy material of his sleeve. "You told me you were dying. Was that a lie too?"

He doesn't answer.

"Wes, I love you. You love me. Don't let them take this from us."

He pries my hands off his arm and takes a step back. "You were a mission. That is all."

"Give me a sign," I whisper anxiously. "Show me that this isn't real. That they're forcing you to say this."

But he just turns and strides toward the door.

"Wait!" I shout, my voice cracking on the word. I see him hesitate. "When I first saw you in Grandpa's cell, you hugged me back. There was no reason for that." I take a step closer to him. "You told me that you loved me. You gave me your watch, Wes. I *know* this is real."

He faces me again, and there's a slight spark in his eyes. *Finally.* But he reaches into his shirt pocket and pulls out the gold pocket watch. "You mean this?"

I reach for my chest, but the watch is gone. "When did you . . . ?"

He last had his arms around me in the cell. While I thought he was showing me a small sign of his love, he was actually taking his watch back. I didn't even notice.

A dull emptiness spreads through my limbs. Is this what going into shock feels like? My legs no longer support my body and I slide onto the floor. Wes stares down at me with what looks like pity. But not love.

It was never love.

"Why did you do this to me?" I spread my hands out on the white tiles and desperately press my knuckles into the floor. It hurts, but I don't care—I want to feel something other than the pain.

"It was my job. I told you someone like me isn't capable of love. You should have listened."

I can't look at him again. Somewhere above me I hear the door open and close.

"Get up," a voice snaps.

General Walker is back, sitting in the same chair. It's like Wes was never here.

I tilt my head up.

"Now you know the truth," General Walker says calmly. He crosses one leg over the other one and hooks his hands around his knee. "The question is what you're going to do about it."

"I thought you were forcing me to become a recruit," I manage to say.

He gives me a thoughtful look. "I have an offer for you to consider. Yes, your first option is to agree to train here as a recruit. But you're right that you are older than any of our other recruits. And you're in a unique position, given that we're holding your grandfather. In exchange for your cooperation, I'm willing to bypass one part of the training process."

"The brainwashing." Now I sound just as robotic, just as emotionless as Wes. "You don't need to break me because you'll kill my grandfather if I disobey you."

"Very good! You are a smart one, aren't you?" His expression darkens. "Your second option: You can refuse, and we will kill you and your grandfather. Because I'm a fair man, I'll let the rest of your family live."

I suck in a breath.

"As a recruit, your main objective will be to stop the nuclear war in twenty fifty. There's nobility in that, Lydia. Don't forget that the Project was created to help people. You could be a part of it."

He smiles at me. It almost looks kind. "I'm giving you something that none of the other recruits have gotten. I'm giving you a choice. You can join us and help save our world, or you and your grandfather can die."

"That's not much of a choice," I whisper.

"And yet it is one." He leans in toward me. "So what do you decide?"

CHAPTER 21

The hallway is freezing. I cross my arms over my chest for warmth. It is always cold in here, or maybe that bitter chill is coming from somewhere inside of me. I can't tell anymore.

I'm still in 1989; I've been at the Center for over a month now. At least I think so—it's easy to lose track of time in this dark, windowless place. The new recruits are housed in the western wing, hundreds of feet below the ground. Every morning we are woken at dawn and sent to training. First, hand-to-hand combat, then karate, then languages, then world history, then wilderness survival. This is only the second stage, they tell us. It will take a year of study and physical conditioning before most of us are ready to start training with the TM.

We're given just enough food to stay alive, and we sleep on bunk beds in a large, open room. There are no blankets or sheets on the beds; too many recruits have tried to kill themselves with them in the past.

No one speaks to anyone else; we learned that lesson quickly enough. All of the kids here are younger than me, and they have already completed the first round of training: the brainwashing stage. Their vacant eyes are unnerving to look at.

So far General Walker has kept his word, and they have not tried to torture me emotionally, to brainwash all my memories away. At least, they haven't done it in the obvious ways. But I don't know how else to describe these endless days. My head hurts from the minute historical facts they pump into it. My arms and legs are bruised from the hours I spend in the fitness center. I try to eat, but the food tastes like paper. I can't sleep. All I hear are the muffled sounds of children crying into their bare mattresses.

I thought that I was alone when I came back from 1944, to a new life where no one knew the real me. But I didn't know the meaning of alone then. *This* is what it's like to truly be alone. To be completely lost in your own mind.

There are still unanswered questions about what happened that I mull over, unable to explain away. Who is the Resister, and what is his rebellion? How did my grandfather find that list? Was I always destined to be a recruit, even before I went back in time to 1944?

Is Wes really dying, or was he lying about that too?

But there's no point in thinking about questions I will most likely never answer.

There's a lot I try not to think about these days. Like how long it will take for my body to start deteriorating too. Will I make the same choice that Seventeen did? I want to say no, but after only a month down here, I'm not sure what I would do. Not anymore.

I mostly try not to think about those people I left behind. Mary and Lucas, who are married and happy in the past. Dean, working as a doorman, with no idea who he really is. LJ, maybe even now being tortured at the Facility in Montauk. My grandfather, shivering in a cell somewhere, probably still drugged. My parents, Hannah, and Grant, never knowing why I disappeared.

And then there's Wes.

Sometimes, when I'm blocking a kick during karate, I'll get a flash of his face in my mind and I'll wonder if he's in these underground tunnels somewhere. Maybe in the housing area where the recruits stay, or even here, watching me train. There are times when I even feel his gaze on me, but I fight against my instinct to turn around and look for him. Instead I jab my elbow into my training partner's throat and listen to them gurgle as they fall to the ground.

It turns out it's easier than you'd think for love to turn into hate.

Because I *hate* Wes. More than I've ever hated anyone.

———

The soldier in charge of my training, First Lieutenant Andrews, informed me that he's expediting the process for me, that he's eager to get me out and into the field. Unlike the other recruits, I'm given small freedoms. Like taking a message from one training soldier to another, and being allowed to walk alone through out-of-the-way, unguarded hallways.

They are not worried about me running away because they know the threat to my grandfather's life keeps me tethered here. And it turns out that Wes was right, at least about one thing. There's no place left to run away to.

I pass a glass door, and I catch a brief glimpse of my reflection. I have been trying to avoid mirrors, afraid of the hollow look in my eyes. But now I stop and stare at the blurry vision of myself. I am stronger, I can see it in the way my muscles curve under the black shirt I'm wearing. But I look like a stranger. Like another one of those robotic recruits, already dead inside. I turn away and hurry back down the hallway.

I thought it would be nice to be by myself for a minute, but somehow it's worse. At least when I'm around the other kids I can trick myself into thinking I'm not quite so alone. But now the solitude is heavy and consuming, and I can't ignore it. I rub my hands together in an effort to create even a small bit of warmth.

The hallway is deserted. Suddenly feeling defiant, I spin

in a small circle. As rebellions go, it's pretty small, but it does make me feel a little better. They cannot entirely control me. I can't forget that.

I hear a noise from up ahead, and I automatically shrink back against the wall. It's footsteps, and they're coming closer. One of our first lessons was on how to conceal ourselves. Because recruits are in and out of the facilities so frequently, we are trained to hide from people we don't know, especially in isolated areas. For one thing, you never know when you might be running into a future or past version of yourself.

This stretch of hallway connects to another corridor, making a T-shape. I doubt there are even any cameras around here, but I still look around for a place to hide.

There is a small alcove to my right and I duck into it. From here I can see the hallway, but anyone approaching won't be able to see me. I make my breathing shallow and low, and I lock my muscles. I am getting better at being still, like Wes always was. But thinking of him makes me want to break something, so I force him from my mind.

The footsteps get louder. Closer. Now I can tell that it's two people, not one, and that they're approaching from the left. Survival training is starting to pay off.

Someone says something in a low voice, and someone else . . . giggles. Down here? It doesn't make sense. I peer around the edge of the alcove and then pull back quickly as two figures round the corner. They stop right in front of me, but just out of sight. I hold my breath as I wait to see what they do.

"We're going to get caught," a girl's voice says. She sounds oddly familiar.

"There are no cameras here."

I press my hands to my mouth. It's Wes's voice. But who is he with?

"It's not safe."

"Stop worrying so much." He sounds like he's on the verge of laughing.

I hear the rustle of clothing, and then the soft sound of lips touching.

I squeeze my hands into fists. He's kissing someone. Of course. It's probably another mission. I bet it's that pretty dark-haired recruit who stared at him in the Assimilation Center. All I want to do is fly around the corner and rip both of their heads off. But I satisfy myself with craning my neck to try and see who she is.

They shift to the right as Wes pushes her lightly against the wall. I suddenly have a perfect view of dark red hair and pale skin.

It's me.

He's kissing *me*.

I can't help gasping, but it doesn't matter—they're too caught up in each other to notice what's happening around them.

They are both wearing the black recruit uniform, and

Wes's hair is shorter than it was the last time I saw him. He sinks his hands into her—*my*—hair and pulls me closer. This other version of me has her eyes closed tight and runs her fingers up his back. He leans away a little and whispers something against her mouth, and she laughs softly.

"I missed you," I hear myself say. "I hate all this pretending."

I want to burst out of this hiding spot, to grab myself and ask how old I am, to demand to know the future, and most importantly, what could ever have changed to make me forgive Wes?

But I can't. If nothing else, the Montauk Project has finally taught me to stop interfering with time. Interacting with a future version of myself would be messing with a line I'm no longer willing to cross.

I watch as they touch each other's cheeks like they're trying to memorize the individual curves and dips. "We don't have much time," she says quietly.

I've never heard my voice in person like this. Mine, but not mine. Lower than I thought it would be, or maybe that's just because of the way Wes is looking at her.

"We're supposed to leave tonight. They don't want us to stay—we're both here in the past right now, remember?"

"I know." His hands tighten on her shoulders. "I don't like to think about that time."

"I hated you."

"I'm sorry."

Future me scrunches up her face and pokes him in the stomach. Love has made her skin glow and her hair shine. There's no way this happy, healthy girl can be the same one I just saw in that cloudy glass door.

Wes grabs her finger and pulls her close again. He presses his lips to her forehead and smiles. He looks lighter than I've ever seen. "Let's go, Lyd. Before they realize we're gone."

She takes his hand and together they walk back up the corridor.

I step out from behind the corner and stare at the now-empty hallway. I press my hand to my chest, the exact place where the pocket watch would fall if I were still wearing it.

For the first time since I arrived down here, I feel a small stirring of hope.